"We had a visitor."

Crandall waited a couple of beats before looking up from his paperwork at Granger. "Who?"

"Clint Adams," Granger replied.

Crandall knew the name. "The Gunsmith? Here?"

"That's right."

"Did you hire him?"

"No, I ran him off."

"You ran off the Gunsmith?" Crandall looked concerned. "He could have been of use to us, Granger."

"Not to me. There's something you should know," Granger replied.

"What's that?"

"He's working for Beverly Press."

"What?" Crandall snapped, surprised. "Can he be bought off?"

Granger shook his head without hesitation. "Not a chance."

"Well," Crandall asked, "have you got enough men to take him?"

Granger laughed. "I can take him, my-self . . . . ."

Don't miss any of the lusty, hard-riding action
in the Charter Western series, THE GUNSMITH

And coming next month:
THE GUNSMITH #60: GERONIMO'S TRAIL

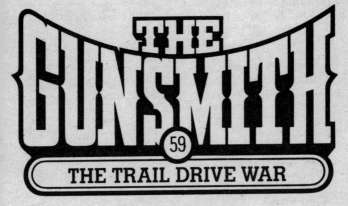

THE GUNSMITH

59

THE TRAIL DRIVE WAR

J. R. ROBERTS

CHARTER BOOKS, NEW YORK

THE GUNSMITH #59: THE TRAIL DRIVE WAR

A Charter Book / published by arrangement with
the author

PRINTING HISTORY
Charter edition / November 1986

ISBN: 0-441-30963-1

Charter Books are published by The Berkley Publishing Group,
200 Madison Avenue, New York, New York 10016.
PRINTED IN THE UNITED STATES OF AMERICA

ONE

Beverly Press was one of Clint Adams' favorite people. She'd aided him twice in the past when he'd really needed it. Now she was calling for him, and he wasted no time in heading for her ranch in Wyoming.

On the way he recalled their shared history. When his big black gelding Duke had been stolen he'd needed a good horse to ride while trying to find him. Someone had recommended Beverly Press as having some good stock. Not only had Clint gotten a horse he could depend on, but he and Beverly had become very good friends.[1]

Then, some months later, Duke had been shot. Once again, Clint turned to Beverly Press.[2]

---

[1] *THE GUNSMITH #28: THE PANHANDLE SEARCH.*
[2] *THE GUNSMITH #31: TROUBLE RIDES A FAST HORSE.*

Both times she'd given him a big white gelding named Lancelot, who had belonged to her late husband and who had never been ridden by anyone but her husband—until the Gunsmith rode him. Clint found the animal to be the most impressive horse he'd ever seen or ridden, next to Duke.

The Press spread was one of the largest in Wyoming. Built up by Beverly's late husband, Brian, it now flourished under her hand. She was a remarkable woman in many ways, not the least of which was her business sense.

As he finally approached the ranch Clint wondered if he was going to have any trouble with Beverly's foreman, a man called Meade. In the past, the two men had not gotten along and Clint was convinced that Meade was in love with his employer.

It was late in the day when he rode up to the front of the ranch house and dismounted. A young man came out of the nearby barn and walked over to him. Clint recognized him as one of Beverly's trail hands, although he didn't recall his name.

"Mr. Adams," the man said.

"Hello—"

"Carl."

"Right, Carl. How are you?"

"Fine, Mr. Adams. Uh, did Mrs. Press know that you were coming?"

"She sent me a telegram, Carl, asking me to come."

"Can't say that surprises me," the man said, taking Duke's reins. "I'll take care of your horse."

"Thanks."

The man nodded and started to walk away.

"Hey, Carl."

"Yeah?"

Clint moved closer so he wouldn't have to shout.

"What did you mean her sending me a telegram doesn't surprise you?"

Carl shifted his feet a bit, and then said, "It may not be my place to say . . ."

"I'd appreciate it."

"Well . . . things haven't been going real well around here, Mr. Adams. You ain't been around for a while."

"How bad *are* things?"

Carl shrugged.

"There's a war brewin' between us and the Crandall spread."

"Crandall? I don't know him."

"He came here last year, started buying out small spreads, making 'em into one big one. Now he's almost as big as us."

"And he's giving Mrs. Press trouble?"

"He wants to buy her out and she won't sell, no matter how much trouble he causes her. Not that lady. She'll tell you what problems he's been causin' her."

"And she needs me for that? What about the sheriff?"

"She'll tell you about that, too."

"Where's Meade? What's he been doing?"

"Meade," Carl said, a funny tone in his voice. He looked down at the reins in his hands and said, "Meade's dead, Mr. Adams."

"Dead? How?"

"Somebody shot him last month."

"Who?"

"Nobody knows."

"One of Crandall's men?"

"He's got plenty of hired guns, any one of 'em could have done it, but like I said, nobody knows for sure."

"Who's the foreman now?"

"Ain't nobody been made foreman since Meade got killed. Things are kind of unsettled around here."

"I can imagine. Thanks for talking to me, Carl."

"That's okay, Mr. Adams."

"Call me Clint."

"I'll take care of your horse . . . Clint."

"I appreciate it."

Clint turned and headed for the house. Meade was dead. He couldn't believe it. He'd expected the big shouldered, red-haired man to be right there in his face as soon as he arrived.

Why hadn't Beverly replaced him, named somebody else or hired somebody else as foreman?

That couldn't possibly be why she had called for him, could it? Naw. He didn't know the first thing about running a ranch.

That couldn't be the reason.

Finding the front door unlocked he walked right in. He knew that Beverly's office was on the first floor of the two-story house and assumed that at this time of the day she would be there. As he approached the room he heard angry voices inside and stopped in the hall to listen.

". . . keep asking you to do something about Crandall and his men and you continue to refuse."

"It's not that I'm refusing, Mrs. Press," a man's voice said. "I just ain't got nothing to pin on him."

"No, but he had something to pin on you—that badge!"

"What are you saying?"

"That talking to you is like talking to a wall, Sheriff, because you're in Dale Crandall's pocket."

"That ain't a nice thing to say, Mrs. Press. I came out here in good faith—"

"I'd like you to leave my house, Sheriff—right now."

"I got to warn you, Mrs. Press. If you or any of your men go near Crandall and his men—"

"My men won't go near his men, Sheriff. My men are trail hands, not gunmen."

"Mrs. Press—"

"Please, get out."

For a moment Clint thought that perhaps he should show himself and help the sheriff find the door, but he decided to let Beverly handle it herself.

"I'm leaving, Mrs. Press, but remember my warning."

There was no reply, and presently a man stepped out into the hall. He was a tall man in his late thirties with bony shoulders and a mustache too large for his thin face. He stopped short when he saw Clint, frowned and then strode past him, heading for the front door.

Clint stepped into the doorway of Beverly's office and saw her sitting behind the desk, leaning back in her chair with her head back on her shoulders.

Beverly Press was a handsome woman in her forties, tall and full bodied and Clint knew her well enough to recognize the fatigue in her posture.

"Hello, Beverly."

She brought her head forward slowly and focused her eyes on him, and then smiled, the fatigue even more evident in that smile and in her face.

"Jesus, it's about time."

"I came as soon as I got your telegram," he said, crossing the room to stand in front of the desk. "I hear you're having some difficulties."

"A few," she said, "a few, not the least of which is a nitwit sheriff who never should have been given his badge."

"And Meade."

"Yes," she said, looking pained, "and Meade. He worked for Brian a long time, Clint."

"I know."

"And he was loyal, to Brian and to me. You didn't like him, but he *was* loyal."

"I know."

They stayed that way for a few moments, silently, she sitting, he standing, and then she stood up and came around the desk to him.

"I'm glad you're here, Clint," she said, putting her arms around his neck and laying her head against his chest. "You can give me what I need, what nobody else around here could give me."

"Beverly—"

"Not that," she said. "Right now I just need somebody to lean on."

He put his arms around her and let her do that. He knew she was a strong woman who would not have let anyone, least of all any of her men, see her wilt under pressure. He felt honored that they were close enough friends that as soon as he walked in the door she would lean on him.

TWO

One of the reasons Clint liked Beverly Press was that she was honest. There was nothing phony or pretentious about the woman, and her wants. Just minutes after they had first met she had taken him to her bed. Now, they left her office and went upstairs.

Beverly's breasts were large and heavy, tipped with big, dusky nipples. She had the full body that Clint preferred and women themselves didn't. They called it plump and he called it comfortable. There was nothing like resting on a well cushioned woman.

"I'm getting fat," she said as he ran his mouth over her nipples.

"You're fishing for compliments."

"Why shouldn't I?" she said. "You never come around unless you need a horse, so my compliments are few and far between."

"If you'd stop being Mrs. Beverly Press the rancher every once in a while and find yourself a man—"

"I've found a man," she said, reaching for him, "but he only comes around when he needs a horse."

"Or when you send me a telegram."

"Believe me," she said, rolling him over, "if I had known it would work so well I'd have sent you a telegram a long time ago."

"You want to tell me just exactly why you sent for me?" he asked.

She began to kiss his chest, murmuring, "Maybe it was just for this."

She worked her way down to his belly and lower. Her mouth covered him, pulled on him, emptied him, and then she mounted him and took him deep inside of her before he could soften.

Even though he felt that her need for sex when he was around was due to the fact that she was otherwise all business, he knew she'd sent for him for more than just this. Right now, however, this was what she needed most. In her own time she'd explain about the telegram.

Now he slid his hands over the cheeks of her generous ass and squeezed as she rode him hard and fast. He moved his hips in unison with hers, allowing her to set the pace.

Did she really go without sex during the long periods of time between his visits? Could she, a woman with an almost insatiable appetite, go that long without it? Or was she insatiable *because* she went so long without?

Or was he flattering himself? As she pushed her full breasts in his face, and as he sucked the nipples, he wondered—as he had wondered before—if Meade wasn't more than just her foreman.

He'd never asked her.

And he never would.

It was three in the morning when they went down to the kitchen for a meal of cold fried chicken, bread and a bottle of wine. Over the meal, she explained.

Dale Crandall had purchased enough land in the area—forcing the smaller spreads to sell out to him—so that he now owned most of the land that bordered her own.

"He wants my spread now."

"You won't sell."

"He's not making it easy for me to hold out, I can tell you that. He's hired gunmen from all over—"

"Do you know any names?"

"Of his men? No, but my men have seen them in action. They're fast, Clint, and they're good."

"How many of your men have been killed . . . besides Meade?"

"Four, and they all looked like a fair fight . . . except Meade. He was ambushed. I think they realized that he was the only real danger to them. You know," she said, laughing ironically, "I thought the men on this ranch were loyal to me, but it was Meade. All along it was Meade who was loyal to me, and they were loyal to him."

"I'm sure some of them stayed, Bev. I saw one of them outside, Carl—"

"Yes, some of them stayed, a lot of them were run off. I hired new men and some of them were run off. I need somebody to hold this place together, Clint. I need a new foreman."

"Me?"

"I need somebody the men will respect, and fear."

"I don't know anything about running a ranch, Beverly."

"Wait," she said, smiling, "there's more. I've got to run two hundred and fifty head of cattle to Texas."

"Why Texas?"

"I've got a private buyer waiting there. He's got a buyer for American beef in Havana, Cuba."

"Isn't there enough beef in Texas?"

"This buyer . . . is an old friend . . . of my husband's. He'll include my beef in with his."

Clint decided to ask Beverly if the buyer was also a close friend of hers. That was her business.

"What about rounding the cattle up and getting them ready?"

"That's what we've been doing for the past four weeks." She shook her head and said, "It shouldn't have taken us that long."

"But it's done," Clint said. "When do they have to be there?"

"When isn't the problem," she said. "*Getting* them *there* is."

"And Crandall's going to try and stop you?"

"He's got to."

"And if he does?"

"I'll be in a bad way, Clint. This hasn't been a good year for me. Even without figuring Dale Crandall into the deal this has been the worst year this ranch has had for a long time." Her tone became urgent as she said, "I need to deliver this herd!"

Clint picked up a cold breast and bit into it. Beverly tried to calm herself, chose a leg and gently nibbled at it.

"All right, you want me to try and find out who his gunmen are?"

"That couldn't hurt, I guess, but that wasn't what I had in mind."

He stared at her as she sipped at her wine, licking it off her upper lip.

"What did you have in mind?"

"I want you to be my foreman."

"Foreman?" he asked.

"And trail boss," she replied, raising her eyebrows at him.

"Trail boss? Jesus, I've never been on a trail drive, Beverly."

"It'll be a new experience for you."

"That's an understatement."

He broke off a chunk of bread, bit into it and chewed thoughtfully.

"Have you got enough men for this drive?"

"That's another problem."

"That's what we need, all right," he said, "another problem."

"Break off a chunk of that bread for me too, will you?"

"Am I on the payroll yet, Mrs. Press?"

"Oh, we have to talk about that too, don't we?"

"About what?" he asked, handing her a chunk of bread.

"Recompense."

"I hope you're not talking about what I think you're talking about."

"I am," she said, grinning. "Salary."

"I'm not taking any pay."

"I pay my foremen—"

"I owe you too much, Beverly, to take your money," he said, cutting her off. He reached for her hand and added, "Though we could discuss some other form of pay."

"I'm sure we can work something out," she said. "I just don't want to feel guilty about dragging you into something without you getting something out of it."

"Cold chicken," he said, gesturing with the half eaten breast, "fresh bread and good wine. What more could a man ask for?"

"Finish eating and I'll show you."

THREE

In the morning they were in the barn. Beverly was looking Duke over, and Clint was doing the same thing with Lancelot.

They turned to each other and spoke at the same time.

"He looks great," Clint said.

"He looks marvelous."

They laughed.

She frowned at both horses and then said, "I hate to admit it, but you might be right."

"About what?"

"About Duke being just a little better looking."

"I never said that," Clint said. "As a matter of fact, I think that Lance is better looking—after all, he's younger—but I think that Duke is the better horse—right now."

"You wouldn't want to take them out and find out, would you?"

"Race them?"

"Sure."

"No."

"Pity."

"Besides, who'd ride Lance?"

She smiled and said, "I would."

He stared at her, then said, "You mean—"

She nodded.

"After the last time you brought him back I decided to try and ride him—and he let me."

She entered Lance's stall and patted the horse's graceful neck.

"We're friends now, aren't we, boy?"

"What about other people?"

She shook her head.

"No, he still won't let anyone else near him. He's still biting off his share of fingers." She rubbed the animal's nose and said, "I'm going to ride him on the drive."

"You'll make a handsome couple."

"Yeah, we will." She kissed Lance's nose and left the stall.

As Clint saddled Duke she explained how many men she needed for the drive.

"I need a dozen more, Clint," she said.

"How many can we get away with?"

She thought a moment, then said, "Eight or nine, I guess, but that's pushing it. I'd feel safer if I had a man for every ten head."

"That's twenty-five men."

"You're a genius, too?"

"I used my fingers."

"I'll bet."

"How many men have you got?"

"I've got a dozen left."

"How many of them are experienced?"

"Eight of them have been with me for six months or more. The other four are recent."

"How many of them can handle a gun?"

"They're cowmen, Clint, not gunmen."

"If we're going to be dealing with gunmen, they should be both, Bev."

"Under ideal conditions, you mean?"

"Yeah."

"Yeah, well, I guess you'll just have to go to town and hire what you can get."

Clint pulled the cinch tight around Duke's great girth and turned to face her.

"I think I'll take a ride out to the Crandall place first."

"What for?"

"Just to see what's what."

"And who's who?"

"Right."

"Be careful, will you? I don't want to lose my new foreman before we even get started."

"That's another question we didn't get to last night, after the cold chicken."

She smiled and said, "Things got kind of heated after the cold chicken."

"I remember."

"What's the question?"

"When do we get started?"

She poked him in the chest with her forefinger. "As soon as you get me some more men."

FOUR

The Crandall house was not yet complete, but Clint could see that it was going to be beautiful. Workmen were still hard at work on half of it, but according to Beverly, Crandall was already living in the finished half.

Clint rode up to the front door and was met by four men. Three of them wore trail clothes and low-slung guns. Dime a dozen hardcases. The fourth man was cleanly dressed and wore brown calf skin gloves on both hands and a gun on each hip. His guns were shiny, well-cared for colts with pearl handles.

The three hardcases stayed on the porch while the fourth man came all the way down.

"Can I help you?"

"I'd like to see Mr. Crandall."

"He ain't hiring."

"I'm not here for a job. In fact, I already have one."

"Really? Ain't that nice."

"Yes, it is. I'm the new foreman over at the Press place."

"You hear that, boys?" the man said, turning his body halfway around. His arms were folded, and his hands were each holding one of his biceps. "This here is the new foreman at the Press place."

One of the men on the porch said, "Ain't much left there to be foreman of."

"Oh, I don't know," Clint said to the man on the porch. "Fact of the matter is, I'm hiring. You wouldn't be interested, would you?"

"I got a job."

"Any of you?" he asked the other men on the porch.

They all shook their heads.

While he spoke Clint took some quick looks around. He saw men he was sure were simply cowboys, but there were other men who resembled the ones on the porch.

Dime a dozen hardcases.

The man with the calfskin gloves was different, though. He was a whole different breed, a top notch gunman who the others would follow instinctively.

And if he was here, there had to be some other top guns along as well, ably backed up by the second raters.

"You want something else?" the man with the gloves asked.

"Am I going to get to see Crandall?"

The man with the gloves shook his head slowly. He was in his mid-thirties, tall and slender, well-groomed and cleanly dressed.

"Not today, Mr. Foreman."

"Well, tell him I came by to pay my respects."

"Who should I say?"

Clint grinned tightly at the man and said, "You know who I am."

The man just smiled and Clint wheeled Duke around and headed for town.

John Granger watched until Clint Adams was out of sight, then turned and ascended the steps.

"Hey, Granger," one of the men called out. "What did he mean you know who he is?"

Granger ignored the man and entered the house. He found Dale Crandall sitting at his desk in his study, sucking on his pipe and filling the room with thick clouds of smoke.

He entered without knocking, which was something Crandall had become used to. Crandall had been forced to accept a lot of things he wouldn't have ordinarily accepted from an employee, but in this case he figured John Granger was worth it.

"We had a visitor."

Crandall waited a couple of beats before looking up from his paperwork. He was a big, florid-faced man in his fifties who owned ranches all across the country, huge spreads that had swallowed up many smaller spreads, whether they wanted to be swallowed or not. The Press spread presented him with his biggest challenge—and John Granger was a necessary evil towards meeting it.

"Who?"

"Clint Adams."

Crandall knew the name.

"The Gunsmith? Here?"

"That's right."

"Did you hire him?"

"No, I ran him off."

"You ran off the Gunsmith? He could have been of use to us, Granger."

"Not to me."

"Don't tell me, you're natural enemies, right?"

"Let's just say I'm less in awe of him than most people are."

"I guess that's your right."

"It's also my right to hire or not hire. You said so yourself."

"You're right about that."

"There's one other thing you should know."

"What's that?"

"He's working for Beverly Press."

"What?" Crandall snapped, surprised.

"He says he's the new foreman."

"Damn," Crandall said with feeling. "Somehow, I didn't think that was her style, hiring gunmen."

"I guess she figures she's got to sink to your level to beat you."

"Granger—"

"Besides, I can tell you that she hasn't hired Adams."

"You mean he's lying?"

"I mean that he doesn't hire his gun out. He's got principles."

"Then what—"

"I'd say it's something personal, a favor, maybe."

"Can he be bought off?"

Granger shook his head without hesitation.

"Not a chance."

"Well, have you got enough men to take him?"

Granger laughed.

"I can take him, myself."

Crandall frowned, not sure whether he believed Granger.

"Do you have enough men?"

"I have plenty."

"Well, send some of them into town."

"For what?"

"Beverly Press doesn't have enough men for a trail drive. Adams will have to go into town to hire some."

"He won't find any."

Crandall stood up, trying to intimidate Granger with his imposing bulk, and failing.

"Send somebody to town and make damn sure he doesn't find anybody."

"All right," Granger said after a moment, "you're the boss."

Crandall noted the sarcasm in Granger's voice as the man with the calfskin gloves turned and left.

He hoped he hadn't made a mistake in hiring the man. Maybe, if he'd been able to get the Gunsmith from the beginning . . .

There had been another man watching the Gunsmith ride away from the Crandall ranch, a tall, black man who now watched John Granger leave Crandall's house and speak to the men on the porch. Two of them then left the porch and headed for the barn, picking up a few more men along the way.

The black man figured it was time to take a ride into town.

John Granger stood on the porch, wondering if

maybe he should have gone into town himself. If he had, either he or the Gunsmith would probably die. There was time enough for that, later.

He wondered about the Gunsmith. In spite of himself he couldn't help feeling pleased that the man—the legend—had recognized him. Still, he had to be careful not to find himself too impressed by the man. That kind of thinking only got you killed.

After all, *he* was something of a legend, himself.

Riding away from the Crandall ranch Clint was thinking about the man with the calfskin gloves.

John Granger.

The man they called "Tenderhands," because nobody knew for sure why he wore those gloves.

The only thing anybody knew about him for sure was that he was a killer, a top-notch gun, and if he was involved in this, it was for sure that this trail drive was going to be no picnic.

FIVE

The nearest town to Beverly Press' place was Deighton, Wyoming, a fairly large town that was still growing, which might have been the reason Dale Crandall had chosen this area to try and establish himself. Of course, Clint knew nothing of Crandall, and would later find out that the man was a major rancher all across the country.

He left Duke at the livery, which delighted the liveryman, and then went over to the Deighton House Saloon. (Briefly, he marvelled at how many towns he'd been in that had a saloon called the "Something" *House*.)

It was fairly early in the day and the place was not particularly busy as he approached the bar. As the bartender put his broom down and came over to get his order, he heard broken glass crunching beneath the man's feet. He was a big, heavy man and the glass made very loud crunching noises.

"What'll it be?"

"Beer."

The bartender crunch-crunched his way back and forth and set the beer down in front of him.

"Must have been some party last night," Clint said, paying for the beer.

"Whataya mean?"

"All that broken glass you're walking on."

"Oh, that," the man said. "Couple of youngsters got liquored up and started feelin' their oats, shot up some liquor bottles. I was bushed last night so I'm cleaning up now."

"When does this place start to liven up?"

"Too early," the bartender said, "so if you don't mind I'll finish sweeping up."

"Go ahead. I think I'll finish my beer and then check in with the sheriff."

"Ha! The sheriff."

"What's the matter with the sheriff?"

"Nothing, except that he ain't much of one." The bartender stopped and leaned on his broom. Clint waited for it to snap beneath his weight. "Why would you want to check in with the sheriff?"

"I'm going to try and do some hiring. That's always good for some trouble, especially when there are people who don't want you to."

The bartender frowned and asked, "Are you working for Crandall, or Mrs. Press?"

"Mrs. Press."

The bartender pointed a finger at Clint and said, "Now that's good for some trouble—but it wasn't always that way. Used to be she had no trouble hiring at all."

"That was before Crandall."

"Yep, before Crandall and his men. Now, anybody hiring on with Mrs. Press takes a chance on getting his head busted—or maybe worse."

"Crandall's men drink in here?"

"When they're in town."

"Well, they'll be in town pretty soon," Clint said, finishing his beer. He turned to leave and said, "Maybe you shouldn't sweep all that glass up, after all. There might be more before you know it."

He walked to the batwing doors, then stopped and turned around.

"What's the sheriff's name?"

"Prendergast."

"You're kidding."

"You'll see," the bartender said. "He had it painted on the door of his office."

"Jesus," Clint said, shaking his head.

The black man rode into town a few minutes ahead of the others. Granger had sent six of his men, and the black man had an idea what they were supposed to do.

He put his horse up in the livery, where he saw Clint Adams' big black gelding. The horse looked even more impressive than he remembered.

He left the livery and started for the saloon, but when he spotted Clint Adams crossing the street he sought refuge in a doorway. He didn't want the Gunsmith to know he was there.

Not just yet.

SIX

Just as the bartender had said, the new sheriff had put his name on the door: T. K. PRENDERGAST, SHERIFF. In all the years Clint Adams had been a lawman he had never seen anything so pretentious.

He entered without knocking. For once, he had no respect for a lawman he had really not even met.

"Can I help you?" the man asked from his seated position behind his desk.

"My name is Clint Adams, Sheriff. I work for Beverly Press."

"Hey, that's right, I saw you out there yesterday, didn't I?"

"You did."

"What's your game, Mr. Adams?"

"I'm Mrs. Press' new foreman, and I'm hiring."

"That's not going to be easy."

27

"I know, that's why I came to you."

The man frowned.

"Why?"

"Because there may be trouble, and I want you to know that I won't be the one starting it."

"If you're hiring for the Press ranch, then you're looking for trouble."

"No, I'm looking for hands, Sheriff," Clint said, opening the door. "Anybody who tries to stop me is looking for trouble."

"Hey!" somebody called from the back room. "Did I hear somebody say they're hiring?"

"Shut up!" the sheriff called out.

Clint closed the door and said, "Who's that?"

"Just a couple of drifters who busted up the saloon last night."

"I'd like to talk to them."

"What for?"

"Maybe they'd be interested in hiring on."

Prendergast stared at Clint for a moment and then said, "I can't let you talk to them."

"Why?"

"Because they're my prisoners."

"For how long?"

"Until they can pay for the damages."

"And how can they do that if they're in jail?"

"That's their problem."

"No," Clint said, walking to the desk, "it's mine. How much are the damages?"

"I don't know. We'd have to go over to the saloon and ask—"

"I was just there," Clint said, taking money out of his pocket. He counted some out and dropped it on the desk. "A few broken bottles, that should cover it." He put the rest of his money away and said, "Let them out."

"You can't do this—"

"Sure I can, Sheriff. I just did. Now let them out, please."

Prendergast glared at the Gunsmith, then took the cell keys out of a desk drawer. He got up, went into the back room and Clint heard the sound of the key in the lock and the cell door swinging open.

As the lawman came back into the room he was followed by two young men in their early twenties. One was husky and curly-haired while the other was taller, slender, with straight hair that curled up over his collar in the back.

"You the fella paid our damages?" the curly-haired one asked.

"That's right. Are you fellas looking for a job?"

"Well, all our money's gone," the other one answered, "so I guess we don't have much of a choice, do we?"

"Not when you consider that you're in my debt."

"Do we have to pay the debt out of our wages?" the curly-haired one asked.

"I'll tell you what. If you take the job I'll cancel the debt."

"You got a deal there, friend."

"Sheriff, would you mind giving my men back their guns?"

"If they're your men," the sheriff said, taking their gunbelts out of a bottom drawer and dropping them onto the desk, "you're going to be responsible for their behavior."

"That's fine with me."

"With us, too," the taller of the two said, strapping

on his gun. Just from the way the two men handled their weapons, Clint had the impression that the taller of the two was more proficient with his than the curly-haired one.

"Okay, boys, let's go over to the saloon and have a drink to seal the deal."

"Great!" they said.

"Thanks very much for your help, Sheriff," Clint said.

Prendergast simply glared at them all until they left.

Outside Clint stopped the two men and said, "You fellas have names?"

"I'm called Trap," the curly-haired one said, "and this here's the Kid."

"The Kid?"

"That's what I'm called," the Kid said. "Sometimes we can't help what we're called."

Clint couldn't very well argue with that, so he dropped the matter.

"All right Trap, Kid, we're going over to the saloon for a drink. Think you can avoid breaking anything while we're there?"

Trap and the Kid exchanged glances and then Trap —who seemed to be the spokesman for the two—said, "We can sure give it one hell of a try."

Crossing the street to the saloon Clint saw two of the men he had seen on the porch of the Crandall house as they were riding into town with four other men. At the saloon, he'd make Trap and the Kid aware of what they were getting themselves in for, give them a chance to get out. He didn't want anyone working for Beverly Press who wasn't fully aware of the situation.

Once again, he did not see the black man standing in a doorway across the street.

"Is that the fella?" one of Dale Crandall's hired men asked.

Tom Luke and Dan Manners were the two men Clint had seen on the porch.

"That's the one," Luke said.

"What are we supposed to do?" one of the others asked.

"Just make sure he doesn't get himself any new hands," Manners said.

"Looks like he may have gotten two already, Dan," Tom Luke said.

"I guess we'll have to go over and take a look," Manners said.

"You boys go on ahead," Luke told the other four. "We'll be along."

As the other four men rode their horses over to the saloon and tied them off outside, Tom Luke turned to Dan Manners.

"Any idea who this fella is, Dan?"

"No, I never saw him before. Why?"

"He and Granger sure seemed to know each other, and he won't tell us who this fella is. I'm just curious, that's all."

"Well, if you're so curious why don't you just ask Granger again?"

"I asked him once and he don't want to answer. That's one man I don't intend to push."

"Well, then let's just go over to the saloon and do what we were told."

SEVEN

Clint, Trap and the Kid each got a beer from the wary bartender and took them to a corner table. Clint sat so that he was facing the entire room, and he noticed that the Kid arranged his chair so that he was doing the same. Trap seemed content to let the Kid watch his back.

"That bartender is looking at us like we bite," the Kid said.

"We did make a little bit of a mess last night," Trap said.

"Only because we were pushed."

"Want to let me in on what happened?"

The Kid grinned and said, "Trap here started paying attention to the wrong girl."

"I can't help it if she likes curly hair."

"Another fella took offense and he had friends, so I had to stand by Trap."

"That's admirable."

"Well, we've been riding together for a few years, now," Trap said.

"By the way," the Kid said. "We didn't get your name. We'd like to know who we're working for."

"You're working for Beverly Press of the Press ranch. We're driving some cattle to Texas. Have you boys worked cattle before?"

"We've worked everything," Trap said.

"You still haven't told us your name," persisted the Kid.

"My name is Clint Adams, and I'm the foreman."

He sat back and watched the astonished looks of recognition on their faces.

"Well," Trap said, and that was that.

At that point the batwing doors opened to admit four men. Clint and the Kid both watched the four men walk to the bar, occasionally stealing glances over to where they were sitting with Trap.

"Friends of yours?" Trap asked Clint.

"I'm not sure, but I'd say they were Crandall ranch hands."

Just then the batwing doors opened and two more men entered, men who Clint recognized.

"*Now* I'm sure."

"They don't look like ranch hands," the Kid said.

"They're not."

"They look like second rate hardcases."

"They are."

Trap looked at Clint and said, "There's something else going on here than just hiring on for a trail drive, isn't there?"

Clint nodded.

"That's why I asked you to come over here for a drink, so I could explain it all to you."

Both of the younger men remained silent and listened as Clint outlined it all for them.

"So there's gonna be some trouble on this drive," Trap said.

"There's going to be *a lot* of trouble on this drive," the Kid said.

"You're both right," Clint said, and then watching the six men at the bar he added, "In fact, we may not even have to wait until the drive for some trouble to start."

Trap and the Kid looked over at the bar.

"Don't tell me," Trap said. "They're here to see to it that you don't get any new hands."

"That's my thinking."

"How many hands do you need?"

"About twelve—but I could make do with eight."

"How many do you have?"

"You two."

"Got a long way to go, don't we?"

Clint nodded.

"We've got the rest of today, and we'll undoubtedly have those six to contend with."

"Do you want us to go out and try to round up some men?" Trap asked.

"I hadn't thought of that, but it's a good idea. The three of us ought to be able to come up with somebody."

"Well," Trap said, "let's do it, then."

Trap and the Kid got up to leave and Clint was impressed with their apparent no-nonsense attitude. Judging from the events of the previous night, however, that attitude apparently came and went. He was going to have to be on the lookout for the times it "went."

"Let's meet back here in three hours," he said.

"Fine," Trap said. "What about our friends?"

"Some of them will probably follow you. Don't start anything, but if they make a move—"

"We understand," Trap said. "Don't worry about a thing."

They headed for the door and Clint watched the men from the Crandall spread. The two who walked in afterward seemed to be in charge, and one of them followed Trap and the Kid with two of the others.

That left three of them covering him.

Idly, he wondered about the two young men with the strange names. No first names, no last names, just "Trap" and "the Kid."

Who were they, really? Were they on the dodge and if so, who from? The law?

Well, for now they were just two young fellas he'd hired for a trail drive. As long as they did their jobs, he wasn't going to pry.

He stood up and walked to the batwing doors, knowing that the three men who were left would follow him. That was fine with him, but the first time they tried to interfere, he was going to have to do something, even if it was only to send a message back to Dale Crandall, and his head gun, John Granger—"Tenderhands."

EIGHT

"We went about this the wrong way," Clint said.

He and Trap and the Kid were seated at the same table in the saloon. Trap and the Kid had returned to find Clint waiting there and told him that they had hired six men. That was fine with Clint because he'd been able to scrape up four. One of the men he'd literally scraped off the floor of another Deighton saloon in town. The word he'd gotten on the man, Manny Jeffers, was that he was a good worker whenever he was sober. He just hadn't been sober for a few . . . months.

All of the men in question had been instructed to meet at the Deighton House Saloon in three hours.

That was five hours ago.

"Oh yeah, I think we went about this all wrong," Trap agreed.

"*We* lined up the men," the Kid said, "and then our friends visited them afterwards and persuaded them not to show up."

"Right," Clint said.

"And that's why they never made a move to stop us from talking to anyone," Trap said.

"Right," the Kid said.

They all looked at each other and then the Kid said, "We went about this the wrong way, all right."

"None of them are going to show up," Trap said.

Clint looked over at the bar, where the six men from Crandall's ranch were talking and drinking, obviously enjoying themselves.

"What do we do now?" the Kid asked.

"Well," Clint said, "we could go out and do it all over again. Maybe we can convince some of them to take the job, anyway."

"And then they'll just do *their* convincing act," Trap said. "I get the feeling that they were a lot more convincing the first time than we were, and they'd probably be more convincing the second time, too."

"You might be right."

"How many head of cows are we driving, anyway?"

"About two hundred and fifty."

"And how many have you got already?"

"A dozen."

"With us three that makes fifteen," Trap said. "We can do it."

"We can?"

Trap looked at Clint and said, "How much do you know about driving cattle?"

Clint hesitated and then admitted, "Not a whole hell of a lot."

"And you're ramroding this outfit?"

"As a favor."

"Can I ask you something?" Trap said.

"Sure, what?"

"You are the Gunsmith, aren't you?"

Clint made a face and said, "Yes. Can I ask you something?"

"Sure, what?"

"What are your names?"

Trap looked at the Kid and said, "We can do it, can't we?"

The Kid shrugged and said, "Sure, Trap."

"All right," Clint said when he realized that his question wasn't going to be answered, "with Mrs. Press, there'll be sixteen of us. I guess we'll give it a try."

They were about to get up when a man walked through the batwing doors—or rather, lurched through.

"Seventeen," Clint said.

"What?" Trap said.

"There'll be seventeen of us," Clint said. "That's Manny Jeffers."

"Well," the Kid said, looking amused, "at least somebody showed up."

They remained seated and waited for Manny Jeffers to see them. The six men at the bar saw Manny Jeffers and two of them moved to intercept him.

"I thought we told you not to show up here," one man said to him.

Jeffers, a small, bandy-legged man who looked to be in his late thirties, peered up at the two men pugnaciously.

"I got me a job waiting for me here," he said.

"No, you don't," the other man said, poking Jeffers in the chest.

"Yes," Jeffers said, "I do," and punched one of the men in the face.

The blow jarred the man's head back, but did little more than that.

"You little sonofabitch!" the man said.

As he drew back his fist to hit the little man Trap grabbed his hand from behind. Clint had not even seen Trap move, but there he was, holding the man by the wrist. The husky man was powerful!

"Hey, what the—"

Trap yanked back on the man's hand and pulled him off balance. When he let go, the man fell.

"This fella is a co-worker of mine," Trap said. He put his hand on Manny Jeffers' shoulder and led him to the table where Clint and the Kid were still sitting.

The two Crandall men—one standing, one on the floor—looked over at Luke and Manners, waiting for their instructions.

Tom Luke and Dave Manners looked at each other, then walked together over to the table where Clint and the others were sitting.

"We talked to *you* already," Luke said to Manny Jeffers.

"Eat shit," Jeffers said.

"You two fellas don't know what kind of trouble you're buying into," Luke said, ignoring Jeffers and talking to Trap and the Kid.

"We're already in," Trap said.

"Then get out," Manners said, "now."

Trap grinned at the man and said, "You heard what he said," indicating Manny Jeffers.

Jeffers said, "Eat shit."

Luke and Manners walked back to the bar. The man on the floor got up and he and his friends followed. They spoke briefly with the other men, then they all walked to the center of the room and faced Clint and company at the table.

"Let's shoot their balls off," Manny Jeffers said.

"Have you got a gun?" the Kid asked under his breath.

"No."

"Then shut up."

NINE

The men standing at the center of the room and the men seated at the table regarded each other quietly.

Finally, the Gunsmith broke the silence.

"I came to town looking for twelve good hands," Clint said to the six men. "I found these three. A drunk and two kids who can't keep out of trouble."

"Thanks," Trap said.

Clint ignored him. He was more concerned with the Kid knowing when to make his move, because he felt most of his assistance would come from him. At closer quarters he'd put his money on the huskier Trap, but when it came to gunplay he figured on the Kid.

"Three men," Clint said, "if you can call them that. Is that worth dying for?"

"You afraid to die?" Luke asked with a cocky grin.

Clint grinned at him and said, "I wasn't talking about me."

The grin fell away from Luke's face and he frowned at Clint. For his money the man was just too confident for somebody who was facing six guns with just a "drunk and a couple of kids."

"I've got a gun pointed right at your belly underneath the table," Clint said, speaking directly to the man he felt was in charge, Tom Luke. "I guess that means that the next move is up to you."

Tom Luke studied Clint Adams and noticed for the first time that both of the man's hands were out of sight beneath the table.

"Well?" Clint asked. "Make up your mind, either turn around and leave . . . or die."

After a moment of silence during which all six men exchanged glances Luke said, "You're crazy."

"The man's not crazy," a voice from behind them said, "He's just good—and he's got more help than he thinks."

The six men all turned around and as Clint did he saw the man standing in the doorway.

A big black man.

Fred Hammer.

"Hammer, what the hell—" Tom Luke said. "You work with us."

"Not anymore, friend."

"Why?"

"Because I didn't like you fellas much to begin with, and because that man over there," Hammer said, pointing to Clint Adams, "could probably kill three of you before you cleared leather."

"Only three?" Clint asked.

"It's been a while," Hammer said to him. "Maybe you slowed down. Anyway, I could just kill the other three, so don't worry."

"Hammer, Granger ain't gonna like this," Dave Manners said.

"Granger," Hammer said, and spat on the floor. "I like him even less than I like you. Now why don't you boys do what the man said. Make your move or leave."

Tom Luke didn't know anything about the man at the table, but he knew all about Fred Hammer, and *Hammer* knew about the man at the table.

"Granger ain't gonna like this," he said, just to get that point across.

"I'll tell you what, Luke," Hammer said. "There's a way we can settle this without anyone dying."

"How?"

"You and your men drop your gunbelts to the floor."

"What?"

Hammer looked past Luke at Clint Adams and asked, "Are you and your men willing?"

"What's he talking about?" Trap asked.

"He's suggesting that we settle this between us without guns."

"Hell, I'm willing," Trap said.

"Me too!" the drunken Manny Jeffers said.

Clint looked at the Kid, who nodded without taking his eyes off the six men in the center of the room.

"Okay, boys," Hammer said, "drop them to the floor and kick them over here."

To bring his point across Hammer produced his gun for the first time.

"Do it!"

The others waited for Tom Luke to unbuckle his belt

before doing the same. The six gunbelts fell to the floor and were then kicked towards Hammer.

At the table Clint brought his hands out empty and said to Trap and the Kid, "Put your guns on that other table."

Trap and the Kid obeyed and then Clint removed his gun from his holster and laid it on the table.

Manny Jeffers had no gun and he was the first one to get up from the table and charge at the six men. Dave Manners, the largest of the six men, clubbed Jeffers to the floor with a big fist but did not see Trap coming at him.

The husky young man swung his fist and struck Manners on the butt of the jaw. The bigger man's head snapped back and Trap punched him in the throat.

Meanwhile, Clint and the Kid rushed forward as a pair and threw their bodies into the fray. They each took two men to the floor with them and from his prone position on the floor Manny Jeffers grabbed the sixth man around the ankles.

Fred Hammer leaned against the wall and watched with amusement the ten men who were now piled up on the floor. One by one they rose to their feet only to begin flailing away at each other. He saw that Clint Adams was doing fine for himself, and that Trap who had made short work of big Dave Manners was making a clean sweep of things. The black man didn't really think that Clint and that young man needed any more help, but with the help they had they had soon disposed of Crandall's men right in the center of the floor, with amazingly, no damage done to the saloon.

"This way," Hammer said, stepping aside to allow them access to the batwing doors.

Clint and the husky young man lifted the six unconscious men one by one and tossed them unceremoniously out into the street. Using his foot, Hammer kicked their gunbelts out after them.

"Well," Hammer said, holstering his own gun, "that's that."

TEN

Hammer came out of the doorway into the room and approached Clint's table, where the triumphant combatants were reestablishing themselves.

"We gave them hell," Manny Jeffers said, one eye almost closed while the other had a cut over it.

"You sure did," Trap said to the smaller man.

The other three—Clint, Trap and the Kid—were relatively unmarked and after they'd buckled their gunbelts back on they sat down.

"What the hell are you doing here?" Clint asked then, looking up at Fred Hammer.

The last time he'd seen Hammer, he and Dan Chow had become a sort of team.[3] Obviously, they had since split up.

[3] *THE GUNSMITH #31: TROUBLE RIDES A FAST HORSE.*

"Well," Hammer said, "I *was* working for Crandall, but I guess I'm working for you now—that is, if you can use me."

"If I can use you?" Clint asked, as if the question were ridiculous. "Fred, this is Trap, the Kid, and Manny Jeffers."

"Eat shit," Manny Jeffers said.

"No, Manny," the Kid said, putting his hand on the drunk's arm, "he's on our side."

"Sit down and have a drink, Fred. We have some catching up to do. Bartender?"

The bartender stuck his head up from behind the bar, where he had taken refuge.

"Bring us some beers, will you?"

"How many?"

Clint looked at Trap, the Kid, Hammer and the drunken Manny Jeffers. Ah, he'd take Manny Jeffers off the stuff tomorrow.

"Five."

"Are these all the men you've got?" Hammer asked.

"You don't look like much, either," the Kid said.

"Settle down," Clint said. "Fred, how long have you been working for Crandall?"

"A week. I was the last one he hired."

The bartender came with the beers and set them down.

"You fellas ain't gonna break any glass today?"

"Not today," Trap said.

"Good."

"Hey," Trap said, "what time does Lori start working?"

"She—"

"Forget it," the Kid said. "You tell him and he'll end

up breaking some more glass.''

As the bartender walked away Trap said, ''You were the one who broke the glass.''

''What are these two talking about?'' Hammer asked.

''Never mind,'' Clint said. ''Who's Crandall got working for him?''

''You know about Granger already because you talked to him this morning.''

''You saw me there?''

''Yes, I did, and I figured you'd be coming to town to look for hands. Knowing Granger, I knew he'd send somebody to keep you company.''

''And you came in to town to cover my back.''

''Somebody's got to.''

''I take it you two are old friends?''

''Acquaintances,'' Fred Hammer said. ''Can we talk, Clint?''

''Sure,'' Clint said. ''Trap, why don't you and the Kid take Manny over to another table.''

''You're the boss.''

''What are you doing ramroding a cattle drive?'' Hammer asked.

''Mrs. Press and I are friends. She asked me to help her out.''

''You don't know nothing about running cattle.''

''She does. She just wants me to help get her and her cattle to Texas in one piece.''

''With these jokers?''

''They're all I've got, them and the dozen hands she still has on her ranch.''

''You know anything about these guys?''

''No, just that they're willing to work for Beverly Press.''

"Do they know what they're going up against?"

"Pretty much—but then again, I don't quite know all that I'm up against. I know about Granger, and I know he's got some second raters—"

"Like Luke and Manners—"

"Those two who just left?"

"Yeah. The others are just arms and legs for hire."

"Well, who else has he got?"

"Willie Strong, Sammy Carter, Dooley Williams—"

"Second raters."

Hammer sipped his beer and then said, "He's got Colin McKenzie and Joe Cantey, as well, Clint."

"McKenzie and Cantey," Clint said. They were first rate guns, just a step below John Granger.

"Those three alone could handle a dozen cowhands with no problem," Hammer said.

"Well, I've got you now, as well, and I have a feeling about the Kid, there."

" 'The Kid?' What kid is that?"

"I don't know. That's all he'll tell me, but he moves like he knows how to use his gun."

"That other fella knows how to use his fists."

"Trap," Clint said. "He and the Kid are partners."

"In what?"

Clint looked over at the two young men and said, "I don't know that, either." He looked at Hammer and said, "I'm glad you're here, Fred. At least I have one man I know I can count on."

"You'll turn my little ole black head with talk like that."

"Fred, what happened with you and Dan Chow?"

"Nothing. We rode together for a while. In fact, I was with him when he sent you that telegram about his sister in San Francisco."

"Yeah, well, I didn't do her all that much good," Clint said, remembering.[4]

"He never blamed you for that. Anyway, we went our separate ways after that. We've crossed trails since then a time or two, but we ain't joined at the hip, or nothing."

"Did you ever learn to throw those little stars of his?" Clint asked. He was referring to the little metal throwing stars that Dan Chow had called *shuriken*. Hammer had been impressed with the way the little Oriental handled them, and had asked to be taught.

"Gave up after a while," Hammer said, shaking his head. "Cut my fingers to pieces with those things. I finally decided just to depend on my gun."

"What brought you here?"

"I heard Crandall was hiring and paying top dollar. When I got here and found Granger, McKenzie and Cantey here ahead of me, I knew something was up."

Clint stared at the black man who would rather call himself an "acquaintance" than a "friend" and then asked, "Why'd you change sides?"

"That's a real interesting question," Hammer said. "I'm not quite sure myself, yet."

"You'll let me know when you are, won't you?"

Hammer nodded.

"You'll be the first to know."

Granger was not happy at the spectacle of his six men dragging themselves back to the ranch. He stood waiting at the foot of the steps to the house, with McKenzie and Cantey standing behind him.

"What the hell happened?"

4 *THE GUNSMITH #36: THE BLACK PEARL SALOON.*

The six men dropped off their horses, nursing their various injuries, and Tom Luke confronted Granger.

"We had them," Luke said, "but that bastard Hammer switched sides on us."

"Hammer? He was in town?"

"He came up behind us and made us drop our guns."

"All six of you?"

"Well, that other fella, the one who was here this morning, he said he had a gun under the table."

"And he didn't."

Looking down at the ground Luke said, "No."

"Did he hire any men?"

"Yeah," Luke said, unhappily.

"How many?"

"Three."

"Three?" Granger asked in disbelief. "And you tried to show them how good you are with a gun?"

"You said you didn't want him hiring any men."

"You're dumber than you look, Luke. What good is three men going to do them?"

"You said—"

"You're lucky Hammer stopped you when he did. Adams would have killed you, easily."

"Adams?"

"Clint Adams."

"The Gunsmith?" Luke asked in disbelief. Suddenly, he felt very cold. He had almost slapped leather against the Gunsmith!

"You didn't tell us!"

"I don't have to tell you any more than I choose, Luke. Remember that."

"Yeah."

"All right, you and these other . . . men go and get cleaned up."

As the six men dragged themselves away, Joe Cantey came down the steps to stand next to Granger.

"What's next?"

"We'll let them start their trail drive. The first chance we get we should be able to scatter their herd, and maybe kill a few of them along with it."

"And the woman?"

"You have qualms about killing women, Cantey?"

Cantey, a tall, cadaverous looking man, said, "I have other things in mind for women than killing them, Granger."

"Yeah, I guess you're right—and this one is not bad looking. Not bad looking at all."

ELEVEN

Beverly Press wasn't all that happy about what she saw riding up to *her house*. Clint Adams had gone to town to hire a dozen men, and he had come back with four.

"What happened?" she asked as he dismounted.

"These are our men," Clint said, indicating the four men who were dismounting behind him. That is, three of them dismounted. Manny Jeffers fell off his horse and Trap and the Kid caught him before he could hit the ground.

"Those—" she began, but Clint held up a hand to stop her.

"You fellas can put your horses in the barn and then get a bunk at the bunkhouse." He turned to Beverly and asked, "Are the men ready to leave tomorrow?"

"They're ready to leave at a moment's notice."

Clint turned back to the four men and said, "We'll be

57

leaving in the morning, so get yourselves ready."

"Can I have a drink?" Jeffers asked.

"Come on, Manny," Trap said, taking the man by the shoulders, "we can talk about it at the bunkhouse."

"I'll take your horse, Clint," Fred Hammer said.

"Thanks, Fred."

Beverly Press' eyes widened when she saw Hammer but Clint motioned her to remain silent.

"Let's go inside."

He followed her up the steps and into the house, where she turned and said hurriedly, "That black man. I've seen him with Crandall's men—"

"I know, I know, but he's working with us now."

"He switched sides? What makes you think he won't switch back—"

"Beverly, it's all right. That's Fred Hammer. I told you about him, remember? When I brought Lance back last time?"

"Oh," she said, remembering. "The black man and the Chinese man? This is the one?"

"Yes."

"Why was he working for Crandall?"

"For the money."

"I can't pay him what Crandall was paying him."

"He knows that. It'll be all right."

"What about those others? Is that all you were able to get?"

"I could go back to town and try again tomorrow, but most of the available men have already talked to Crandall's men. I don't know if I can get them to change their minds."

Looking tired Beverly said, "Let's go into the study."

He followed her down the hall and into the study, where she sat at her desk.

"Those men," she said, "they're not enough. My God, one of them is the town drunk."

Clint hadn't known that Manny Jeffers was the town drunk, but he was hoping that when Jeffers dried out he'd be able to work.

"Look, Beverly, Hammer's a good man, and so are the other two. We can dry Jeffers out. You've got a half a dozen men who have been with you a while, and the others are experienced cowmen."

"What about Crandall's gunmen?"

"You let me worry about that," he said, putting both hands on the desk and leaning forward. "Hammer and I can handle anyone Crandall has."

"You mean, you still want to try this with just the men we've got?"

"That's what I mean—that is, if you're willing."

Beverly Press stiffened her back and stood up, saying, "I'm more than willing."

"All right. Do you think you'd be able to rustle something up for dinner? I'm kind of hungry."

"I'm kind of hungry, too," she said, coming around the desk and putting her hands on his hips, "but you can take care of that after I feed you, I guess."

"I suppose I could give it a try."

Over dinner Clint told Beverly everything that had happened in town.

"I guess you're lucky your friend Hammer came along," she said.

"It saved some gunplay, that's for sure."

"I don't think we're going to be that lucky, though, not between here and Texas. There's bound to be gunplay."

"I'd have to agree with you there," Clint said, "especially since Crandall has John Granger ramroding his outfit.''

"Who's John Granger?"

"He goes by the ridiculous name 'Tenderhands,' " Clint explained, "although he's probably no more to blame for that than I am for being called the Gunsmith."

"Why do they call him that?"

"He wears calfskin gloves on both hands."

"Is he . . . very good with a gun?"

"He wears two of them, and he's real good with both of them."

"As good as you?"

Clint shrugged.

"Who else does Crandall have working for him?"

"Some second rate guns and cowmen, but there are two other men we have to worry about: Colin McKenzie and Joe Cantey."

"Gunmen?"

He nodded.

"And good ones."

"We don't have anyone else but you and Hammer who can handle a gun."

"That might not be the case, Beverly. Those two young fellas I told you about, Trap and the Kid. I get the feeling the Kid can handle his gun pretty well."

"Have you seen him?"

"No, but I've seen the way he moves, and I saw him when we were standing off Crandall's men. His eyes never left them. No, I'd be pretty surprised if he couldn't handle his gun fairly well."

"That makes three and three, then," Beverly said. "That pits the rest of our men against the rest of Crandall's, and we're outnumbered about five to one."

"Well, I've been up against better odds," Clint said, "but I've faced worse, too."

"I haven't," Beverly said, cleaning the plates off the table. "This is going to be a new experience for me."

"Have you ever been on a trail drive before?" he asked, suspiciously.

"Quite a few," she said, and then added, "When I was a bit younger. It's . . . been a few years."

"You haven't forgotten what it was like, have you?"

"No," she said, staring off into space, "you don't forget that."

"Come on," he said, standing up and taking her hand, "let's go upstairs."

In bed later, Beverly gave Clint a quick course in how a trail drive was put together.

The trail boss—Clint, with her at his side—would ride ahead of the drive, riding back occasionally to check in with his men. The chuck wagon came next, pulled in this case by four mules. Off to one side would be the horse wrangler, who was in charge of the remuda—that is, the fresh remounts. Along the way the men would have to change mounts from time to time.

"We can give that job to Manny Jeffers," Clint said, interrupting her lesson.

"Do you think he'll be able to handle it?" she asked, doubtfully.

"I'll have Hammer ride along with him until we're sure he can."

"Hammer seems very competent," she said. "Shouldn't we have him riding with the main body of the herd?"

Clint shook his head.

"I don't want Hammer to be concerned with the herd at all. I want him to keep an eye out for Granger and the rest of Crandall's men. We can't afford to be surprised by them. We'll concentrate on keeping the herd together and Hammer will concentrate on keeping us alive."

"That reminds me," she said. "I've told all of the men to make sure they're armed."

"That's good thinking. Even if they can't hit anything the noise they'll make might help. Okay, let's go on with the lesson, teacher."

Behind the chuck wagon, she explained, would come the point riders. It was their job to lead the cattle, and very often for this purpose they would use a lead steer.

Next, where the herd widened out, would come the swing riders, and towards the center of the herd the flank riders. At the end would come the drag riders, and these were usually the men who were newer to trail drives.

"That's where I should be riding," Clint said.

"Maybe that's where we should put your two friends, Trap and the Kid."

"They say they've worked cattle before."

"But it's all my men do. I think we need the more experienced men in the key positions. Do you think your friends will mind?"

"I don't think so," Clint said, not bothering to point out that they weren't really his friends.

"They'll have to eat a lot of dust."

"That's what they're getting paid for. By the way, how much are they getting paid?"

"The men will get twenty-five to thirty dollars a month, depending on how experienced they are. I'll have to figure out what it comes to at the end of the drive."

"That's not much."

"You'll be getting ninety dollars a month."

"No, I won't."

"Let's not argue."

"Okay," he said, reaching for her, "let's not argue."

Clint lingered over Beverly's firm, full breasts, suck-ling the nipples until they were so erect and sensitive that she had several small orgasms.

Next he slid down between her legs and used his tongue on her clit until it too was erect and the orgasm she experienced then was anything but small. She cried out and lifted her hips off the bed and it was all he could do to grab ahold of her firm buttocks and hold on.

She returned the favor later by burrowing her face into his crotch and licking his cock until it was standing tall and thick. She slid her lips over the spongy head, laved it with her tongue and than began to suck him, caressing his testicles at the same time. Several times she brought him to the brink of orgasm only to stop.

"You're a tease, woman," he finally said, and pulled her atop him. They each moved their hips and suddenly he was buried inside of her to the hilt.

"Oh, yes," she moaned, sitting up on him and grind-ing her crotch down against him. She put her hands flat on his chest and said, "This is going to have to last us until the end of a long trail drive, Clint Adams, so I hope you're ready for a long ride right now."

"I may be ready tonight," Clint said, reaching up to caress the smooth flesh of her breasts, "but I don't know if I'm going to be ready in the morning."

"I won't wear you out," she promised, and then leaned over and whispered into his ear, "too much."

TWELVE

Beverly Press' men were already out with the herd, getting it ready to travel. She and Clint met Trap, the Kid, Manny Jeffers and Fred Hammer out in front of the house to give assignments.

Jeffers looked miserable, since he hadn't had a drink since the night before.

"Can I have a drink before we start?" he asked.

"You're going to have to go without a drink for a while, Manny," Clint said.

The little man stared at him and said, "What?"

"I'll explain it to you, Manny," Hammer said, "while we're working the horses."

"You boys don't mind riding drag, do you?" Clint asked.

"Do we have a choice?"

"Hammer's going to be up front," Clint explained,

"and I'd like you boys to watch the back."

"Sounds like a good idea," Trap said.

"No problem," the Kid said.

Clint turned to Beverly and said, "Let's get this drive going."

They got their horses and rode out to where the rest of the men were watching the herd. Clint looked out over the cattle and shuddered at the thought of tons of beef being driven out of control. Naturally, if Granger were going to try anything, a stampede would make the most sense.

Clint moved up alongside of the Kid before he could get into position and asked, "Can I talk to you for a minute?"

"Sure," the Kid said. To Trap he said, "Catch up to you in a while."

When they were alone the Kid said, "What's on your mind?"

"You are. I get the feeling you know how to handle that gun pretty well. Am I right?"

"I get by."

"No, I don't mean you 'get by.' I mean you're pretty good."

"I don't have a big rep, if that's what you mean."

"A reputation doesn't mean a thing, Kid."

"You can say that?"

"I think I have more of a right than most people to say that, yeah."

"What do you want to know, Clint?"

"Aside from Hammer and myself I don't know of anyone else I can really count on if it comes to gunplay. I want to know if I can count on you."

The man Clint knew only as "the Kid" stared at him for a few seconds and then said, "Yeah, Clint, you can count on me—and for what it's worth, you can count on Trap, too. Nothing fancy, mind you, but you can count on him."

"Okay," Clint said, and then again, "okay. Maybe we can talk a bit between here and Texas, Kid."

"Why not?"

"Good. Okay, get into position and let's get this thing rolling."

As the Kid rode away to join Trap, Fred Hammer came riding over.

"You want to tell me what my real job is, boss? I mean, you don't really want me playing wet nurse to the town drunk, do you?"

"Your job is the most important one of all, Fred."

"What's that?"

"You get to watch my back and make sure nobody puts a bullet into it."

"Well, I done that before."

"Just do it as well this time and we'll be all right."

"You got it."

Clint rode over to where Beverly was talking to the cook in the chuck wagon. He was a large man with huge forearms, and he was apparently unhappy about something.

"What's the problem?" Clint asked, dismounting.

The man looked at him and Beverly said, "Pete, this is Clint Adams. He's going to be the trail boss on this drive."

"What's the problem, Pete?" Clint asked, again.

"I didn't know I was gonna be cooking for no niggers," the man said, sullenly.

"Is that a fact?" Clint said to Beverly, then turned to the cook and asked, "You don't like black men, Pete?"

"Ain't never known one was worth a damn."

"Well, I tell you what. You don't have to like Hammer, all you've got to do is cook for him."

"I don't even know what they like. I can't cook no black food."

"Well, since we've only got one on this drive, Pete, why don't you just make what you always make, and he'll have to eat it whether he likes it or not."

The man's face suddenly brightened and he said, "Yeah, that's right. Let him eat what we eat, huh?"

"Right, Pete," Clint said, giving the man a conspiratorial look. "That'll fix him."

Clint took Beverly's arm and led her back to her horse and held Lancelot's head while she mounted.

"Well, you passed your first baptism of fire," she said, looking down at him.

"What do you mean?"

"Handling the cook. He's usually the stubbornest most cantankerous member of the drive."

"Pete?"

She shook her head and said, "Whoever the cook happens to be."

"Is that a requirement for the job?"

"They're usually lousy cooks, and everyone lets them know. That'd make anyone cantankerous."

"Can he make coffee?"

She nodded.

"Strong and hot."

"Then he's got a friend in me. Are we ready?"

"I am when you are," she said, and then added with a grin, "trail boss."

THIRTEEN

One of the things Beverly told Clint they would have to watch closely was the herd's instinct for home. They would have to be closely guarded and briskly driven for the first few days, until the danger of their breaking away and heading for home passed. Of course, driving the herd hard meant driving the men hard, as well.

The first three days passed uneventfully. At daybreak the men would rise for breakfast, and the last two men on watch would stay with the herd until someone finished breakfast and relieved them. Then the horses would be rounded up and saddled and, after the cook had cleaned up, the drive started again and continued until about eleven. At that time the cattle were allowed to graze while the hands had lunch. Again, men were left on watch and ate when the first to finish relieved them.

69

From there the men who were to stand first guard on the herd that night moved on with the chuck wagon to the next campsite so that when the herd came in they were prepared—and rested enough—to hold it until the first relief of the night.

The only potential problem happened on the first night, during dinner. Clint watched carefully as Hammer approached the chuck wagon for his dinner.

Pete had fixed some stew and biscuits and when Hammer held out his plate and the two big men's eyes met, Clint tensed, ready to step in if he had to. He noticed Beverly watching, too.

The moment passed, however, with Pete wearing a superior grin and Hammer a puzzled frown. Pete watched as Hammer tasted the food and seemed disappointed when the black man continued eating without complaint.

The third night when Hammer held his plate out Pete said, "How do you like the food, so far?"

Hammer stared at the man and then said, "I've had better."

That seemed to satisfy Pete, but Clint wondered for how long. The cook was big enough to possibly give Hammer some competition, if he was anything more than a talker. When he found out that Hammer ate the same food as everyone else, it was going to be interesting to see his reaction.

"How are we doing?" Clint asked Beverly when he sat beside her with his plate.

"What are we making, ten, twelve miles a day?" she asked.

"About that."

"Then we're doing fine," she said, but her tone belied her words.

"You don't sound happy about it."

"I'm worried. We're doing *too* well. Where are Crandall's men? Why haven't they tried anything yet?"

"Don't worry, they will. Crandall hasn't hired those men for no reason, believe me."

"How can you be so calm?"

"I'm just waiting, Beverly," he said. "I'm doing what you hired me to do."

"You certainly are. You've taken to this trail boss position quite well."

"Thanks, but I don't think I've ever worked as hard as these past three days."

She laughed.

"And this is just the beginning."

"You're holding up quite well, yourself," he said. "In fact, you're a damn distraction to the men. Why don't you wear some baggy clothes, or something."

"I'm the boss, Clint," she said. "I can wear whatever I want."

"Well, don't be surprised if somebody jumps you in your bedroll some night."

"Well," she said, grinning, "I only hope it's some night soon."

There had been some question in the minds of both Clint and Beverly—though neither had voiced it—about whether her men would resent Clint as trail boss. Any possibility of that, however, seemed to be dispelled when Clint took his first turn at watch on the first night, and took a turn the two nights after that.

On this night he was on watch with Trap and the Kid, and the three circled the herd, keeping an eye out for strays, and for Crandall's men.

The three of them were rarely in the same place at the

same time, but two of them occasionally crossed paths, and at one point when Clint and Trap passed each other, Trap stopped.

"The Kid told me what you talked about before the drive started."

"You two tell each other everything."

"We've been riding together for a long time," Trap said. "Knowing each other has helped us keep each other alive."

"I can't argue with that," Clint said, "but if we're going to keep each other alive, I'd like to know more about you two."

"What's to know?"

"Your names, for instance."

"I'd have to think about that," Trap said. "But there is something you should know about the Kid."

"What's that?"

"He told you that you could count on him if it came to gunplay, but he didn't tell you how good he is with a gun."

"And how good is he?"

"He's the best I've ever seen—bar none. I know your reputation, Clint, but sight unseen, you against the Kid, I'd have to take the Kid."

Trap seemed especially confident in his friend, and to Clint that meant that there was some truth—a lot of truth—to what he said.

"I know something about unwanted reputations, Trap," Clint said. "How could a man as fast as you say the Kid does *not* have one?"

Trap started his horse forward and said over his shoulder, "I never said he didn't."

No, Clint thought, but the Kid had said he didn't.

Who was telling the truth?

FOURTEEN

At breakfast Hammer carried his plate over to sit next to Clint.

"What's the holdup?" he asked.

"What do you mean?"

"They should have hit us by now, don't you think?"

"Granger's smart," Clint said. "He's making us wait for it. You wouldn't happen to have heard any of his plans while you were there."

"Not a one. I was only there a week, and some of the other men didn't appreciate my being hired."

"Why were you hired?"

"Granger and I have worked together before."

"Often?"

"Too often," Hammer said, moving his food around on his plate. "I really didn't want to take the job, but things have gotten a little tight lately."

"Why? I don't mean why have things gotten tight, I mean why did you hate to take the job?"

"After the last time we worked together I swore I'd never work with him again." Hammer dropped his fork onto his tin plate and set the plate down on the ground. "The man is not right in the head, Clint. Something isn't working right up here," Hammer said, tapping his temple.

"That's true of a lot of men like Granger."

"I know, I know. I make my living with my gun, Clint, and I've known a lot of men who do, but to us it's a profession. It's what we do to make money. Granger does it because he really likes it. He likes to hurt people, and then he likes to kill them."

After a moment Clint said, "Well, you've answered your own question, then."

"Which question?"

"About what the holdup is."

Hammer frowned, picked up his plate and said, "I don't get you."

"Chances are he'll do the same thing with us," Clint explained. "First he'll try and hurt us, and then he'll try to kill us."

"You may be right."

"How's Manny holding up?"

"Better than I thought he would. He wants a drink bad, but since there's none to be had he's doing pretty well. I thought he'd be screaming by now."

"Maybe he's not really a drunk. Maybe he just drinks to . . . forget something."

"We all do that at one time or another."

"Some of us more than others."

Hammer nodded, put some food in his mouth and then made a face.

"This is awful. What's wrong with this cook, anyway? He keeps asking me how I like the food."

Tom Luke dismounted and walked up to Granger, who was having a cup of coffee by the fire with Joe Cantey and Colin McKenzie.

"What are they doing?" Granger asked.

"Same as every morning," Luke said. "They're getting ready to break camp."

"Fine."

"Hey, when are we gonna do something. You're not gonna wait until they get to Texas—"

"Shut up, Luke," Granger said. "I don't have to explain anything to you."

"Okay, okay. Can I have a cup of coffee?"

"Sure."

Luke poured himself a cup and then made a move as if to sit down with the other three men.

"Have it somewhere else," Granger said.

Luke stopped short, stood up and then walked away with the coffee.

"Couldn't you have gotten a few more pros?" Joe Cantey asked, "instead of a bunch of tinhorns like him?"

"I'd have to pay pros more money," Granger said, "and then we couldn't split what I'm gouging Crandall for salaries, could we?"

"Well, when *are* we gonna do something?" Cantey asked.

"Soon," Granger said, "soon."

"Why don't we just take the herd from them?" McKenzie asked.

"Because we're going to do it my way, that's why," Granger said. "We'll hurt them a few times, whittle them down little by little before we finally move in and take the herd.''

"What about the woman?" Cantey asked. "Crandall didn't say anything about the woman being on the drive.''

"No, he didn't," Granger said. "I guess that'll make it just that much more interesting, huh?"

Cantey and McKenzie exchanged glances. They had worked together many times, and very often with—or for—Granger. It was no secret between them that neither of them liked Granger much, but they were always paid the best when they worked for him.

Still, neither man felt comfortable around the man known as "Tenderhands."

"What are you going to do about the Gunsmith?"

"The Gunsmith," Granger said, staring off into the sky. "Now he's really going to make this interesting. I've always looked forward to facing him. I think I'm going to save him for last.''

"Your best bet with him would be to backshoot him," McKenzie said.

"What?" Granger said, glaring at McKenzie. "Shoot him in the back?"

"That's the only way to handle somebody like him," McKenzie said. "The way McCall killed Hickok."

Granger stared at McKenzie for a long time and then said, "Don't ever suggest that to me again, McKenzie, do you hear? Never again, or you'll wish you had shot *me* in the back.''

FIFTEEN

At the end of the first week Clint Adams' behind ached like never before, along with every muscle in his lean body.

He had begun to make it a habit of riding back often and talking to the men. He didn't tell anyone, but it made him uncomfortable to be riding *ahead* of all those cows.

He had gotten to know most of the men by name, and felt that if anyone had harbored any resentment towards him when the drive started, they didn't anymore.

He usually worked his way slowly towards the back where he rode alongside Trap and the Kid.

"We're starting to wonder if you really need us," Trap said when Clint joined them. Both men were wearing their bandanas over their mouths and noses.

"It *has* been a week," the Kid said.

77

"We'll make Colorado tomorrow," Clint said.

"What's that mean?"

Clint shrugged.

"Granger is obviously waiting for something. Maybe that's it."

"And maybe this fella Crandall doesn't want Mrs. Press' spread as bad as she thought."

"Maybe," Clint said. "It couldn't be that you fellas are tired of eating dust, could it?"

They both looked at him and then Trap tugged his bandana down so Clint could see his smile.

"Now that could be, yeah."

"I'll see if I can't get you boys a raise."

Clint worked his way back up the herd on the other side until he was riding alongside Beverly, again.

"Everything all right?" she asked.

"Fine."

"You really don't like riding up here ahead of all that beef, do you?"

He looked at her and said, "You're a pretty smart lady, aren't you?"

"No, I just feel the same way. In fact, my husband did, too."

"We haven't talked much about your husband."

"No, we haven't."

For a few moments they rode in silence and he was content to let the subject drop because he thought that was what she wanted. Soon, though, she began to talk.

"He was older than me by some fifteen years and I used to hate it when he went off on drives. We lived in Texas originally, you know."

"I didn't know."

"Yes, we only moved up to Wyoming about two years before he was killed."

"How was he killed?"

She looked at him and said, "In a stampede. It was the way he always felt he would die."

Clint knew about that. He had always felt—and still did—that he would die from a bullet. His fear—the only one he would admit to—was that the bullet would come from behind, like Hickok.

"He was too old to be on a drive, but you couldn't tell him that. It was even more puzzling because he hated drives, but he felt that he couldn't send his men and his foreman on a drive without going with them."

"He must have been almost sixty."

"He was sixty—and he hated that, too." She was silent for a few moments, then she turned to him and said, "I never told anyone this, but I think he went on those last couple of drives hoping that he would be killed."

Again she lapsed into silence and Clint didn't quite know how to break it. The only thing he could think of saying would sound callous.

Finally, Beverly said, "I guess he got his wish."

Damn, he thought, that's what he'd been going to say.

After they broke for lunch Clint went over to talk to the cook.

"Pete, how's it going?"

"Fine," the big man said. "You want some more before I clean up?"

"No, I've had enough."

He'd had more than enough. What he *had* eaten felt like a stone in his belly. Just when he thought the food couldn't get any worse, Pete surprised him.

He had asked Beverly why she'd hired such a lousy

cook and she had said, "I had everyone else lined up, but not a cook. He was all I could get on such short notice."

"Hey, that nigger's eating my food without complaining. Did you notice that?"

"He complained to me," Clint said.

"Really?" Pete said, looking eager. "What'd he say?"

"He said he didn't know how anybody could eat such terrible food."

"Hey, we got him good, huh?"

"Sure, Pete, we've got him."

"Bet he wishes he had some good black food, huh?"

"Listen, Pete, I want you to ride up ahead and make camp for us. I'm going to send the wrangler with you. Okay?"

"Sure, Clint, sure. I'll have dinner waiting for you when you get there. How's that?"

Clint smiled and said, "That's fine. Oh, by the way, do you have a gun?"

"Sure, in the wagon."

"Keep it at hand."

"You still think that Crandall's men are gonna try something?"

"It's possible."

"Well, if they do, I'll be ready."

"Good, Pete, good."

Clint walked away from the man and found Manny Jeffers. The little man looked terrible, but he had looked a lot worse two days before.

"How you doing, Manny?"

"Not bad, Mr. Adams," Jeffers said. "I can't remember the last time I went this long without a drink."

"Are you complaining?"

"No, sir. I think maybe after this I won't go back to it."

"That's good, Manny."

Since he'd been off the whiskey and gotten cleaned off a bit Clint was able to see that Manny Jeffers was younger than he had thought. It had been the liquor that made him look older, and though he still looked like a man in his early thirties, Clint felt that he was a lot younger than that. He wondered what had happened in the young man's life to drive him to the bottle.

"Listen, Manny, I want you to take the horses and go with Pete, the cook. You'll go up ahead and make camp for the night."

"Sure, Mr. Adams. Whatever you say."

"Have you got that gun I gave you?"

"I've got it."

Clint had given Jeffers a gun at the beginning of the drive.

"Okay, keep it handy. At the first sign of trouble, start shooting."

It never occurred to Manny to wonder why, if he was expecting trouble, Clint would be sending him and Pete on ahead alone.

"I will. You can count on me."

"I know I can, Manny."

As Clint walked away he was intercepted by Hammer.

"What's up?"

"I'm sending Manny and the cook on ahead to make camp."

"That'd set them up for Granger and his boys."

"I know."

"Want me to go along?"

"No."

"You're putting them out there as bait?"

"Yes," Clint said. "I'm getting a little tired of playing Granger's waiting game. I'm going to give him something he can't refuse."

"Just you and me gonna follow?"

"No, I want you to stay with the herd."

"I thought I was supposed to watch your back."

"If we both leave the herd they'll hit it instead of taking the bait."

"You're not going alone, are you?"

"No, I'll take Trap and the Kid. I'll have somebody else ride drag for a while."

"I'd feel better if I was going with you."

"Stay with Mrs. Press, Hammer. I want to make sure I don't have to worry about her."

"Well," Hammer said, "that's damn near the only time I've ever been flattered."

SIXTEEN

It was about a half hour from darkness and Clint, Trap and the Kid were watching the camp from ahead. They had crossed into Colorado about an hour earlier. It had been Clint's idea to stay ahead of Manny and the chuck wagon, figuring that Granger and his men were following the herd from behind. If he sent men after the chuck wagon they'd have to circle the herd. The safest place for Clint and the two younger men to watch from would be ahead of everyone.

They were on the other side of a grassy knoll, taking turns keeping watch. At that moment, it was Trap who was watching, while Clint and the Kid hunkered down by the horses, sharing some beef jerky.

"We haven't had much chance to talk alone, Kid."

"No, we haven't."

"Want to tell me about yourself?"

"There's nothing to tell."

"How long have you been calling yourself the Kid?"

"How long have you been calling yourself the Gunsmith?"

Clint made a face and said, "I don't."

"Well, I didn't start calling myself the Kid," the younger man said.

"Trap thinks you're pretty handy with your gun."

"So do you."

"No, I mean he says that he knows you're good. In fact, he says you're the best he's ever seen."

"Trap talks too much."

"Who says?" Trap asked, joining them.

"I do," the Kid said.

"I only speak the truth," Trap said. He nudged the Kid with his foot and said, "Your turn."

The Kid got up and walked up the knoll to keep watch.

"What makes you so curious?" Trap asked Clint.

"It's a trait I come by naturally," Clint said. "It's aggravated by the fact that you fellows don't seem to have names. I mean, real names."

"We have real names," Trap said, "but you wouldn't recognize them."

"Well, obviously someone would, or you wouldn't have retired them."

"That's an assumption."

"It sure is."

"Hey!"

They both reacted to the Kid's voice immediately, and joined him on the top of the knoll.

"Riders," the Kid said, pointing, "there."

Clint saw about a half a dozen riders approaching the place where the chuck wagon and remuda were camped.

"Let's get down there."

"They'll see us coming," the Kid said.

"If we wait too long we won't be able to get down there in time. We'll circle around, then come at them from a blind side." He turned to face both men and said, "We're not going to shoot unless they do, but if that happens I want them hit. I don't particularly want them killed, but I want them going back in pieces."

"A message," Trap said.

"Right."

"Let's move then," the Kid said. "Those riders are coming fast."

They ran down the knoll and mounted up.

"Who do you think we're up against?" Trap called out.

"Granger won't be sending his top men. Probably the same ones we saw in the saloon."

They were riding hard after that, with no opportunity for conversation.

Clint hoped they'd get down there in time to save their bait.

Pete, the cook, saw the riders first and called them to Manny Jeffer's attention.

"Are they from the herd?" he asked.

Manny squinted and said, "I doubt it. They're riding their horses too hard. Get your gun."

Pete ran to get his gun from the wagon.

"Are they Crandall's men?" he asked.

"I'd say yeah," Manny said, taking his gun from his belt. "I'd say we were put out here as bait, my friend, but let's show these shit eaters that bait can fight back.''

The six riders were perilously close now and Manny Jeffers raised his gun and fired. The cook followed his example. The two men weren't coming close to hitting anyone, the firing of their guns held the attention of the approaching riders, and warded them off enough so that Clint, Trap and the Kid arrived in plenty of time.

Clint's first shot jerked the lead rider from his saddle, and suddenly the others became aware that they were in trouble.

The Kid's first shot killed another man, while Trap fired twice before he hit someone. The remaining three riders turned their horses and began to flee.

"I want at least one of them to make it back!" Clint shouted.

Trap looked at the Kid and said, "Put up your gun."

Calmly, the Kid raised his gun and fired at the fleeing men. He put one bullet in a man's leg, another in a second man's shoulder. Clint pulled his rifle out, sighted and fired, taking the third man from his saddle.

"That'll do it," he said, lowering his rifle. He looked at the Kid and said, "Good shooting."

The Kid holstered his gun and shrugged.

They rode up to Manny and Pete, both of whom were unharmed.

"We showed them," Manny said. He looked directly at Clint and added, "Bait can bite, huh, Mr. Adams."

"Pete," Clint said, "make some coffee, will you?"

Over coffee they all watched Pete concoct his latest delight.

"Do you think we should ride back to the herd?" Trap asked.

"I don't think so," Clint said. "By time those two

get back to Granger, the herd should be here. Granger's going to want to evaluate the situation before he makes another move."

The Kid looked over at Manny Jeffers, who looked like a new man.

"How you doing, Manny?"

"I'm doing great," Jeffers said, grinning. "I ain't felt this good in a long time."

"You didn't mind being put out as bait, Manny?" Clint asked.

"Mr. Adams, when you been nothing but shit on for as long as I have, anything is an improvement. Anytime you wanna use me as bait, you feel free. Just do me one favor."

"What's that?"

"Let me know next time."

When the herd came in Clint breathed a sigh of relief. In spite of what he had told the others, he'd been a little nervous about leaving the herd.

Hammer rode up to him and asked, "Trouble?"

"Nothing we couldn't handle," Clint said. "How about you?"

"None at all. How did your two friends do?"

"They did fine," Clint said, "just fine."

"What about Manny?"

"Came through like a pro."

Beverly rode up alongside Hammer and looked down at Clint.

"How did everything go?" she asked.

"According to plan," Clint said. "Get down and I'll tell you about it. It might keep your mind off Pete's cooking."

Dismounting and handing Lance's reins to Hammer

she said, "This had better be some story."

The two remaining men of the six Granger had sent after the chuck wagon rode back into Granger's camp and fell off their horses.

"Jesus," McKenzie said.

One of the men was Tom Luke, the other one McKenzie didn't know by name. Luke had been shot in the arm.

"They were waiting for us," he said, sitting on the ground, clutching his wounded arm. The other man was rolling around, holding his leg with both hands. Blood was pumping out from between his fingers, indicating that an artery had been severed.

Granger came walking over with Cantey and stared down at the two men.

"What happened?" he asked Luke.

"They were waiting for us," Luke repeated.

"There were six of you."

"They were on us before we knew it, shooting the others right out of the saddle."

"Who?"

"Adams, and two others."

"*Two* others?"

"Well, there was the cook and the wrangler."

"A *cook* and a *drunk*?"

"They had guns!"

"I've got a gun, too," Granger said. Before Cantey and McKenzie knew what had happened Granger had taken out his gun and fired once into Luke's head. The other man looked up from the ground in time to take one in the face.

"He would have died, anyway," Granger said,

holstering his gun, "and Luke kept messing up."

"Sure, Granger," McKenzie said.

Granger looked at Cantey and said, "How many men have we got?"

"Thirty, give or take."

"Adams outsmarted me this time," Granger said, pulling his gloves on tighter. "I guess he earned his rep, but I've earned mine too—and he's gonna find that out."

SEVENTEEN

They doubled the guard that night and Clint wanted to keep either himself and Hammer or Trap and the Kid on at all times.

While Trap and the Kid were out there with two other men, he, Hammer and Beverly had a cup of coffee around the fire.

"Granger ain't gonna like being outsmarted," Hammer said. "He's gonna be looking to get even."

"He's not going to go off halfcocked, however," Clint said. "Granger's a pro. He'll be satisfied to go through this whole drive one down as long as he can come out on top in the end."

"You don't think he'll come after us again until after the drive?" Beverly said.

"No. If his job is to keep you from delivering your beef, that's what he'll do. I only meant that he's not going to come tearing in here after us just because we picked off six of his men."

"I hope not. If he did that we'd lose control of the herd for sure."

"And the chances were good that he'd lose a lot more men, both to us and under the hooves of the herd," Clint explained. "If Crandall wanted your herd that bad he would have had you burned out at the ranch."

"Jesus!" she said, shocked.

"What?"

"The ranch is virtually unprotected. I had no one to leave behind to watch it."

"That's okay. He's not going to do anything that overt, not even with the sheriff in his pocket."

Clint wasn't all that sure he was right, but Beverly didn't need that preying on her mind for the remainder of the drive. Hammer gave him a look which he acknowledged with a shrug.

"Well, I guess I'd better turn in," Beverly said, dumping the remnants of her coffee in the fire. "I'll see you gentlemen in the morning."

"Good night," Clint said.

As she walked away Hammer stared after her and said, "That's one tough, determined lady."

"Yeah."

"I got an idea."

"Let's hear it."

"Granger's out there somewhere with a large group of men. He can't hide."

"And we could find him, even in the dark?"

"You're a mind reader."

"What would we do when we found them, Fred?"

Hammer shrugged and said, "Kill Granger."

"Just like that?"

"The way you'd kill a mad dog," Hammer said, "before he can bite you."

"I couldn't do that."

"I could."

Clint shook his head.

"Sending you out to do it would be the same as doing it myself."

"Give him a shot at you, Clint, and he might not miss."

"That's a chance I'll have to take."

"Well, he's taking the same chance."

"I've never seen him in action."

"I have."

"Is that why you're warning me?"

"I'd warn him too."

"Do you have an opinion as to what will happen if and when we meet?"

Hammer thought a moment, then said, "It will be very interesting."

During the watch Hammer and Clint split up, Clint riding with Carl and Hammer with one of the other men, Zeke.

"Can I speak frankly, Mr. Adams?" Carl asked.

"If you'll call me Clint you can, Carl."

"All right, Clint. In the beginning, when we found out that Mrs. Press was hiring you to be the foreman and trail boss, some of the men objected. Some of them even resented you."

"And now?"

"You've proven yourself to them. You've worked as hard on this drive as any of us, and they appreciate that."

"I see."

"I just thought you'd like to know that."

"I appreciate it."

"We just wanted you to know that anything we could do, you know, for Mrs. Press, you just let us know. We're not afraid of Crandall's men."

"You should be."

"What?" the younger man said, looking confused.

"It's okay to be afraid, Carl," Clint said. "It makes you careful, and being careful keeps you alive."

"You mean, you're afraid?"

Clint looked at the young man's face in the moonlight.

"I'm still alive, aren't I?"

EIGHTEEN

"We're short," Pete the cook told Clint the following morning.

"How did that happen?" Clint demanded. "We should have been stocked for twenty-four men, Pete, and we don't have *that* many."

"I don't know how it happened," Pete said, "we're just short. Maybe a lot of the men have been having second helpings?" the cook suggested.

Clint didn't seriously think that was part of the problem, but he kept that opinion to himself. Besides, he didn't think Pete himself was serious. The man couldn't have illusions that warped about his own cooking.

"What's wrong?" Beverly asked, coming up from behind Clint.

"Pete says we're short on supplies."

"How could that be?" she asked. "We should have been stocked for—"

"I've gone through all that," Clint said, cutting her off. "We'll just have to get some more supplies so we can feed the men we've got." Clint turned to Pete and said, "Make me a list, Pete, and make damn sure you check it twice. Understand?"

"Sure, sure, I understand."

Pete went to work taking inventory and making a list.

"I'm going to need some extra money," Clint said to Beverly.

"You've got it. Where are you going to go for the supplies?"

"The next town is Madison. I'll take one of the extra horses to use as a pack horse and go into town for the supplies. You can keep the herd going and I'll catch up to you in a few days."

"Why should you go?" Beverly asked. "Why not send a couple of men?"

"I don't want to take two men off the herd, Beverly, and neither do I want to send two men out there to be set upon by Granger's men."

"Well, what about you?"

"Granger will think twice before sending some men after me," he explained, "and he won't come after me himself. Not yet, anyway."

Again, he wasn't being completely honest with her. Granger might very well send some men after him, but Clint felt better about exposing himself to that danger than any of the other men.

This time, though, Beverly Press wasn't buying one bit of it.

"I think you just don't want to send anyone else out there alone."

"Look, Beverly," he said, trying to explain his reasoning, "you've got men here who drive cattle. That's what they do best. If I send them into town and they have to go up against a couple of gunmen, then they're out of their element. Handling gunmen, that's what I do best."

"Take Hammer with you."

He shook his head.

"Granger knows and respects Hammer. I've got to leave him here with you."

"Then take someone, for God's sake." She was becoming exasperated.

Clint decided to relent, even if it was just to put her mind at ease.

"All right," he said, putting his hand on her shoulder to calm her. "I'll take either Trap or the Kid with me. Their talents as cowboys won't be missed."

"I just can't understand how something like this could have happened."

"I have one suggestion as to how it might have happened." Clint said, thoughtfully.

"What's that?"

"First, tell me who bought the supplies in the first place."

"Pete. As the cook on the drive that's part of his job. I told him how many men we had, and he should have bought enough for everybody—and more."

"Well, while I'm gone I'll just have Hammer keep a close eye on Pete."

"You mean you think he didn't order enough, on purpose?" she asked, shocked. "But, that would mean that he's working for Crandall."

"All I'm saying is that it's one possibility, Beverly—a very good possibility."

"So why don't we just fire him on the spot? Or better yet, leave him behind."

"No, not yet. I'll just have Hammer watch him closely from now on."

"What if he does something to the food? Puts poison in it, or something?"

Clint looked at Beverly and, grinning, said, "How much worse could the food be?"

"If we get rid of him I could do the cooking."

"Well," he said, "that answers that question."

Clint left it to Trap and the Kid to decide which one would accompany him, and when they suggested that they both go, Clint vetoed the idea.

"I want one of you here to watch Hammer's back, and one with me to watch mine."

"Well, we've got Hammer and all the rest of the men here," Trap said, "and there'll only be two of you out there. I guess you'd better go with him, Kid."

Clint got Duke and the pack animal ready and met the Kid, who was all mounted up and ready to go.

Hammer came over and Clint said, "Watch out for everything, Hammer."

"Between Trap and me we got it covered, Clint. Just watch your asses out there in the open."

"We've got that part of it working on our side," Clint said. "Out in the open like that they won't be able to surprise us."

"And with that pack animal you won't be able to outrun 'em."

"That's it, Hammer," Clint said, "look on the bright side."

"What the hell are they doing?" Cantey asked.

He and McKenzie and Granger were watching the camp from high on a ridge, Cantey looking through a telescope.

"Hand me that looking glass," Granger said to Cantey, who handed it over.

Granger focused and saw Clint Adams and another man riding away from the camp leading a third horse, but instead of riding south, to scout ahead, they were riding to the east.

"They found out they're short of supplies," Granger said. "Adams is heading for town with another man."

"What town?" McKenzie asked.

"The next one, Madison," Granger said.

"Do you want us to go and take them out?" McKenzie asked.

Granger looked at McKenzie and asked, "Can you take the Gunsmith?"

"I, uh—I doubt it."

"What about you?" Granger asked Cantey.

"I don't think so."

"Then if I send you after him the chances are you won't come back, and I need you."

"Are we going to take the herd while he's gone?" Cantey asked.

"We're going to take a piece out of them," Granger said, "just a piece. When he comes back he'll find that we've taken a bite out of it."

McKenzie and Cantey exchanged glances behind Granger's back. They didn't agree with his methods—they would have been a lot more straightforward about it—but he was getting paid by Crandall, and they were getting their money from him.

"Whatever you say, Granger."

Granger turned slowly and gave them both a long

look each. When he spoke it was to McKenzie.

"Pick out four of the boys and send them into Madison ahead of Adams."

"What do you want them to do?"

"The first chance they get I want them to isolate the other men from Adams," Granger instructed, "and kill him."

"What the hell do you think you're doing?" Clint demanded.

He and the Kid were just about ready to leave when Beverly came riding up on Lance.

"I'm going with you."

"Beverly—"

"Don't argue with me, Clint," she said, cutting him off quickly. "I've decided that I can't trust you with my money, so I'm going to go along and make sure that you spend it right."

"Are you afraid I'll spend it on liquor and women?"

"I don't know what you'd spend it on, but I'm going to be there to make sure it isn't liquor and women."

Clint looked at the Kid, who simply shrugged and said, "She's the boss."

"He's got the idea," Beverly said.

"All right," Clint said, "but on one condition."

"What's that?" she asked, suspiciously.

"That the minute we ride out of here, I become the boss. The whole time we're away, what I say goes."

Beverly considered the deal and then said, "All right, I agree."

"Too quickly, if you ask me," Clint said, the suspicion his now. "Much too quickly."

NINETEEN

Madison was a small town with not much chance of getting any larger, but at least it had a general store, a livery and a hotel, and that was all Clint and the Kid needed.

Oh yeah, and a saloon.

They put the horses up in the livery and started for the hotel, which they had located during the ride in.

"I'm a little surprised," the Kid said on the way.

"About what?"

"That we got here without any trouble."

"What kind of trouble were you expecting?"

"I don't know. A half a dozen men maybe could have run us down and taken care of us."

"Not Granger's style. If the headlong rush were what he favored, he would have used it with the herd."

"I don't get it. He was probably hired by Crandall to

101

make sure the herd didn't get to Texas, and he could have done that the first day."

"I don't think Crandall would be able to tell Granger how to go about it. From what I know of "Tenderhands," as they call him, he pretty much does things his own way."

"He must have seen us ride away," the Kid said. "If you were him, what would your next move be?"

"I'd send some men into town ahead of us."

"How many?"

"Three, maybe four."

"To take care of all of us?"

"No," Clint said, "you."

"Why me?" the Kid asked. He wasn't surprised or insulted, he was just asking for his own information.

"Granger knows me, he doesn't know you. He'd send some men here to wait until we split up and then take care of you."

"Why just me?"

"Because he'd want to save me for himself."

"What about me?" Beverly asked, speaking for the first time.

Clint looked at her and said, "For all we know, he's saving you for himself, too."

She made a face and said, "He wouldn't have a prayer in hell."

"And you might not have a choice. Let's get those hotel rooms."

They got two rooms at the hotel, making no secret of the fact that Clint and Beverly would share one, and then discussed splitting up.

"We could go over to the general store, and then the saloon."

"I could meet you at the saloon," the Kid said. "You

don't have to hold my hand, Clint. You were just guessing, anyway.''

Clint went to the general store while the Kid went over to the saloon. They agreed that Clint would arrange for the supplies, which they would pick up in the morning, and then meet the Kid at the saloon.

Beverly, on the other hand, wanted to do some errands of her own, and agree to meet both men at the saloon.

There were four men in the saloon who had arrived in town just minutes ahead of Clint and the Kid. Three of them were seated at a table while the fourth kept watch at the batwing doors. He reported the arrival of Clint Adams and the other man to his three partners, and then when he saw the second man walking towards the saloon he left his position at the doors and told the others, ''He's coming over. Get ready.''

When the Kid entered the saloon he saw the four men sitting together at the table.

''Good guess, Clint.''

Clint crossed over to the general store and was about to go in when he saw four horses tied to a hitching post nearby. He glanced at them briefly, looked away and then decided to walk over for a look before going into the store.

He found what he was looking for on the first horse, then on all of them. One could have been chance, but all four was too much of a coincidence.

The Crandall brand.

The Kid considered leaving the saloon and avoiding

trouble, but if the four men had been sent there specifically to take care of him, how much of a chance was there of avoiding them completely? Surely, if he left they'd go looking for him.

He walked up to the bar and ordered a beer. Briefly he wondered how long they'd wait before making their move.

He didn't have long to wait.

He watched in the mirror as the four of them got up and walked over, splitting so that there were two of either side of him.

If they decided to take him with their hands he'd have little chance against the four of them.

He could only hope that they'd try with their guns. He'd have more of a fighting chance that way.

". . . don't think I like his face," one of the men was saying as Clint was about to enter the saloon. The Kid was standing at the bar, having a drink, and there were two of each of Granger's men on either side of him. Clint stayed outside, listening.

"Look," the Kid said, dropping his hands below bar level, "if you fellas are trying to get me riled you're doing a piss-poor job of it. If you want me to draw on you, make the first move."

With that the Kid backed away from the bar so quickly that the four men were left standing at the bar, flatfooted and confused.

"Let's go," the Kid said.

"All four of us?"

"If you want to go and get some help, I can wait."

The four men exchanged glances, waiting for someone else to make the decision. The same thought was going through each of their minds. "This nut *wants* us to draw on him."

That wasn't natural.

"Come on, come on, boys," the Kid said, "I can't wait all day. I haven't killed anybody all week."

Clint could see that the men at the bar wanted no part of a man who was pushing them to draw on him. They stood there, undecided about what to do, and then one of them finally made a decision.

He started away from the bar towards the door.

That made up the minds of the others.

That is, of two of the three others.

One by one they all started for the door, and Clint relaxed, but then the fourth man made a decision of his own.

His hand streaked towards his gun, hoping to catch the Kid off guard. Clint saw it and was about to step inside when the Kid moved.

He fired once, killing the man who had gone for his gun. The shot forced the other three to go for their guns, but they never had a chance. The Kid just kept firing, his bullets punching home with unerring and deadly accuracy.

By the time Clint stepped inside, they were all dead— and he had witnessed the fastest move he'd ever seen.

The Kid holstered his gun and stared at Clint with his arms folded.

"Don't be impressed," he said. "The fourth man killed them all when he went for his gun. The others weren't prepared to draw."

Clint stared back at the Kid and said, "I'm impressed."

TWENTY

"Wait a minute," Jim Benson, Sheriff of Madison, Wyoming said, "let me get this straight. *You* never touched your gun at all?"

"That's right," Clint Adams said.

He and the Kid were in the sheriff's office, where Benson had taken them from the saloon after the four bodies had been removed.

"You killed all four of them?" the sheriff asked the Kid, still unable to accept it.

"That's right, but one of them drew first."

"I'm not questioning that," the lawman said. "The bartender backs you up on that part. I just can't see one man outdrawing four."

"I explained that," the Kid said. "The other three weren't ready for their friend's move. If they were, I wouldn't have had a chance."

Clint didn't necessarily agree with that statement, but he kept his opinions to himself.

"*You're* the Gunsmith, right?" Sheriff Benson said to Clint.

"Yes."

"And who are you?"

"Nobody."

"I need a name, son," the sheriff said. "If you don't give me one, I'll have to hold you."

"Smith," the Kid said.

"First name?"

"Thad."

"Is that your real name?"

"You asked me for a name," 'Smith' said, "and that's the one I'm laying claim to."

The lawman stared at the Kid for a few moments, then wrote the name down on a piece of paper.

"When are you fellas planning on leaving town?"

"We *were* planning to leave in the morning," Clint said, "but with everything that's happened I never got a chance to go to the general store, and it's after six o'clock. I guess it's closed by now?"

"Yeah. If you'll promise me that you'll be out of Madison by late tomorrow morning, I'll get them to open for you."

"Sheriff," Clint said, smiling, "you've got a deal."

They found Beverly and explained what had happened. She too was suitably impressed by the Kid's feat, but he still insisted that circumstances had lent him more than a helping hand.

After giving their order to the disgruntled owner of the general store Clint, Beverly and the Kid went to find someplace to have dinner. They had been barred from the saloon by the sheriff, but he hadn't said they couldn't have dinner in some restaurant.

They found one on a side street and both ordered a bowl of stew that put Pete's to shame.

"I don't know if I can go back to eating Pete's cooking after this," the Kid said.

"You may not have to," Clint said, and explained to the Kid what he had suggested to Beverly the day before.

"Maybe the best thing would be to let him alone and keep an eye on him."

"That's what I've been thinking."

"If he makes a false move you can always close in on him."

"Beverly is afraid that he might do something to the food, perhaps going as far as poisoning it."

The Kid looked at Beverly and said, "From what Clint has said about Granger I don't think he'll do anything that obvious."

"My thinking exactly," Clint said.

"Well . . . good. I'm glad we're in agreement."

"On most things."

"What do you mean?"

"I think you could have taken those four even without the excuse you've been giving them."

The Kid did not reply at first, then said simply, "I won't argue with you. You're the man with the rep."

"Yeah, so I am, but a rep doesn't mean anything when you're facing another man with a gun."

"What are you saying, that you think I'm faster than you are?"

"No, I didn't say that," Clint said, "but you're faster than anyone I've ever seen. In fact, you might just be faster than me."

"But you're not saying I am."

"On any given day one can outdraw another," Clint said. "Let's leave it at that."

The Kid shrugged and said, "Fine."

Again, Clint was impressed with the Kid. He'd been baiting him, trying to see if he'd claim that he *was* faster than Clint, and the young man made no such claim. In fact, the question did not seem to matter to him at all.

The Kid seemed to have all the confidence in the world in his own ability, so much so that he didn't have to walk around talking about it.

That was possibly the most impressive thing of all about the young man.

Except for the way he'd gunned down four men in the saloon.

After dinner they went to their hotel rooms to get some rest. They wanted to get as early a start as possible in the morning, and once again the sheriff had added his assistance, arranging for the owner of the general store to meet them well before his usual opening time.

"What was all that business about him being faster than you?" Beverly asked.

He explained and she said, "So he passed your test."

"He's smart and he's fast and he's not cocky."

"And maybe he reminds you of someone? Yourself, at that age?"

He hadn't realized it before, but that was true. The Kid did remind him of a young Clint Adams.

"You're too smart for your own good, lady," he said, putting his arms around her.

He kissed her and she attacked his clothing, unbuttoning and unbuckling in a frenzy.

"You think I came with you to watch my money?" she said. "I came for this!"

She had his pants off and knelt in front of him, fondling his swelling penis and heavy balls while she herself was still fully dressed. She stroked his erection until it was rock hard and then slid her lips over the head. She suckled him, continuing to fondle his testicles as she did so, and soon—too soon—he exploded.

"If that's all you came for," he said after he got his breath back, "it's all over."

"No, it's not," she said, standing up and beginning to undress. "Not by a long sight."

Later, while Beverly dozed in his arms, Clint admitted that his curiosity about the Kid—and by association, Trap as well—was at its peak. The first chance he got he wanted to send a telegram to Rick Hartman in Labyrinth, Texas, to see what Rick—a veritable fountain of information—could turn up on the two just from their description, and from the name the Kid had given the sheriff.

By the end of the drive, Clint hoped to have his curiosity satisfied.

"What are you thinking about?" Beverly asked, stirring. "Me?"

"What else would I be thinking about?"

"You're pitiful," she said. "I hand you a lie and you pounce on it."

Instead of denying it he turned over in bed and pounced on *her*, and she didn't object a bit.

TWENTY-ONE

Instead of rejoining the herd on the third day, Clint, Beverly and the Kid made it back by the evening of the second day. There were no incidents during their ride back, part of which took place at night when they realized that they might catch up early. They figured that was because Granger had no way of knowing that his four men would not be coming back. He'd have to wait until at least the third day before deciding that something had gone wrong.

When they came within sight of the fire Clint called out that they were coming in, to avoid being shot by an over-eager cowboy on watch. Riding into camp, he could feel the tension in the air.

"What's wrong?" he asked immediately.

Hammer said, "We had a little trouble. Step on down and have a cup of coffee and I'll tell you about it."

"Where's Trap?" the Kid asked immediately.

"On watch," Hammer said. "He's okay."

"I'll take care of the horses and get the supplies stowed with Pete," the Kid said, and Clint nodded.

They had agreed during the ride back that the Kid would keep a close eye on Pete whenever Hammer was unable to.

Clint stepped up to the fire and accepted a cup of coffee from Hammer. Beverly, tense and nervous, anxious to find out what happened, turned down a cup.

"All right, what went wrong?"

Hammer hesitated for a moment, as if looking for the right words, and then said, "We lost two men."

"How?"

"We had the watch doubled up, as usual, but they got in and killed two of the men."

"How?" Clint asked, again.

"They had their throats cut," Hammer said, and Clint could see Beverly wince.

"Who'd we lose?" she asked.

"Two of your regular men," Hammer said. "The other men said their names were Roy Dade and Carl Skinner."

"Carl Skinner?" Clint said, frowning. He looked at Beverly and asked, "Is that . . . Carl?"

"Yes."

He hadn't known Carl's last name.

"That's right," she said, "you knew him better than the others, didn't you."

"A little," he said, and then said, "Damn!"

He sipped the coffee and scalded his mouth, which didn't improve his mood any.

After a moment he said, "Hammer, who does Granger have who could have slipped in on a four man watch and killed two of them?"

"You mean, if he didn't do it himself?" Hammer shrugged. "Could have been any one of the men I didn't know, but I'd put my money on Cantey. He handles a knife pretty well, and he spent some time with the Indians when he was younger. He'd be able to do it."

"Right, Cantey," Clint said, remembering what he knew about the man. "All right, we'll have to triple the watch. Six men."

"Already done," Hammer said, "but Clint, these men are gonna be worn out standing extra watches and then driving cattle all day."

"Can't be helped. I'm going to go out and stand a watch now. Hammer, you and the Kid will be part of the relief. I want two of us on at all times."

Hammer leaned forward and said, "What about Pete? Who's gonna watch him?"

Clint frowned, running the names of the other men through his mind, then made a decision he hoped he wouldn't regret.

"Have Manny watch him."

"Jeffers?"

"We have to use everyone, Fred."

"You're the boss."

Hammer went off to talk to Manny Jeffers and Clint moved to the other side of the fire, next to Beverly. He reminded her that Granger had lost four men in Madison.

"Somehow that doesn't make me feel any better, Clint," she said. "Two of my men is not an even trade for a hundred of his."

"I agree, Beverly, but Granger's down ten men now, eight dead and two wounded. The odds are closer, and we may have gotten rid of the possibility of an all out attempt to stampede the herd.''

"I don't know if my ranch is worth the lives of two men, Clint."

"They knew what the chances were, Beverly," he told her, "and they apparently thought it was worth it. Don't cheapen their deaths by saying it wasn't."

"I'm sorry," she said, "I'm upset."

"I know. You have every right to be. Get some rest and then—"

"No," she said, cutting him off. "I want to stand a watch."

"Bev?"

"You said it yourself, Clint," she argued. "We need everybody we've got."

He studied her face and saw that she was determined to do this.

"All right, but you'll ride with me."

"Fine."

"Get your horse."

As she started away he called out to her and she stopped and turned.

"Don't use Lance for the watches, Beverly. He'll stand out too much."

"All right."

Clint decided to take another horse himself and give Duke a well deserved rest. By the time Beverly returned with a horse, Clint had a bay mare from the remuda all saddled and ready.

Hammer came over as they were mounting up and said, "Manny is on Pete."

Hammer gave Beverly a long look, and then Clint a short one, but did not comment on the fact that the "boss" lady was taking a watch.

"Fine."

"The Kid told me what happened in town," he said. "Odds are tightening up."

"Some."

"Might make Granger change his plans."

"That's fine with me," Clint said. "If we can influence his decisions then we're in control."

"I guess that's one way of looking at it," Hammer said. "I'll be out to spell you in three hours."

"Fine."

"Be careful."

"Always."

The Kid came over then and asked, "Want me to come along?"

"Not this watch, Kid. Take the next one with Hammer, in three hours."

"Right."

Clint and Beverly rode out and spelled two of Beverly's men. Their appearance was a break in the routine Hammer had established, but they would reorganize the watch the next day. Clint just wanted to get out there right away and couldn't very well blame Beverly for feeling the same. After all, they were her men.

He'd have actually been disappointed in her if she *hadn't* insisted on taking a watch.

TWENTY-TWO

"It's been three days," McKenzie said to Granger. Cantey stood by, listening. "Three days since we gave up on those men coming back. That means that we took out two of theirs while they took out four of ours. That's bad odds, Granger."

"I'm not worried," Granger said.

"I am," McKenzie said, aware that he was questioning a man he essentially feared.

"Are you worried, too?" Granger asked Cantey.

Cantey shrugged.

"I'm not getting paid to worry," he said. "That's what you're getting paid to do."

"We have a big bonus riding on this thing," McKenzie reminded Cantey.

"You'll get your bonus, McKenzie," Granger assured the other man.

"How?"

"Look," Granger said, "they're standing triple watches, right?"

"Right."

"Let them stand them for a few more nights and they'll be asleep in the saddle by day. When that happens they'll be easy pickings."

McKenzie wasn't so sure anymore that Granger had any kind of a plan. He thought the man might be making it all up as they went along. Losing ten men to two was not his idea of a plan that was working—especially when Granger had killed two of his own men who had only been wounded.

Granger's hand on McKenzie's shoulder made the man start in surprise.

"Take it easy, McKenzie," Granger said, gripping McKenzie's shoulder harder than was necessary. "Your bonus is virtually in your pocket. Trust me."

When he said, "Trust me," Granger squeezed McKenzie's shoulder so hard that the man winced from the pain.

The pressure sent a message. "I'm the boss, don't question me!"

And McKenzie read it very clearly.

"Whatever you say, Granger."

"That's a good boy," Granger said, releasing the hold, "a good boy. Now why don't you mount up and go and check on the herd for me."

"Sure," McKenzie said glumly.

John Granger and Joe Cantey watched the man mount up and ride out, and then Granger moved closer to Cantey, tugging on his gloves and flexing his hands.

"He's getting nervous."

"Anxious."

"Same thing," Granger said. "I may want you to kill him somewhere along the way."

Cantey didn't answer.

"His attitude might spread to the rest of the men."

Cantey knew that the rest of the men were already somewhat upset at having lost ten of their number—especially since they all now knew that the Gunsmith was down there with the herd, but he kept his silence.

"His part of the bonus would be yours, then."

Cantey digested that little bit of information for a few seconds and then said, "You're the boss, Granger."

"Yes," Granger said, "I am."

TWENTY-THREE

"I don't know how long the men can keep this up," Hammer said.

He was riding alongside Clint, who knew the fatigue the men were feeling because he felt it, too.

"I know."

"And it looks like Granger's not going to get tired of playing his waiting game."

"I know," Clint said, again.

"You know, Clint, I'm falling out of the saddle and you know how much stamina I've got," Hammer said, immodestly. "Imagine how the rest of these men are feeling."

"I don't have to imagine it, Hammer."

They exchanged hard looks for a few moments, and then Hammer said, "No, I guess you don't. Don't mind me, Clint, I'm just running off at the mouth."

"With good reason though, Hammer," Clint said. "Maybe it is time we took the offensive."

"What have you got in mind?"

"Nothing beyond that," Clint said. "I know we've got to do something, but I don't know what, yet."

The death of young Carl was eating at Clint and it was one of the reasons that he wanted to do something now.

"If you have any suggestions, I'm open for them."

"Not a one," Hammer said, "but if I come up with something I'll let you know."

Hammer went back to join Manny Jeffers and the remuda, and Beverly Press rode over alongside Clint.

"What was that about?"

"Just an exchange of ideas," Clint said.

"What did you two come up with?"

"We found out that neither one of us has any idea what to do next." Immediately he realized that was the wrong thing to say. "Don't worry, by tonight one or both of us will come up with a course of action."

"You mean we're not going to wait for them to make their move?"

"I think we've waited long enough, Beverly," Clint said. "We're all ready to fall out of the saddle, and *that's* what Granger is waiting for. We're not going to give him the luxury of waiting any longer. It's time for us to make something happen and get on with the business at hand."

She nodded and said nothing. Clint took a moment to study her. As weary as she was—as she *had* to be—she had never once complained, not about being tired. He knew she was second guessing herself constantly about making this drive, and he was more determined than ever to deliver her and her herd to her buyer in Texas.

They rode in silence for a while, and once again—as had happened many times since the drive started—he became accutely aware of the herd behind him.

And suddenly he had an idea, one that should have occurred to them long ago.

TWENTY-FOUR

"You want to do what?" Beverly asked in disbelief.

"Did he just say what I think he said?" Hammer ked in the same general tone.

"He said it," Trap said, and the Kid simply nodded d waited for more.

Clint had kept them all off watch to explain his idea them, and they had reacted just as he had expected.

"I want to turn the herd," he said, again.

"You want to go back the way we came?" Hammer ked.

"Just a short ways."

"How short?" Beverly asked.

"To wherever Granger and his men are camping."

"And then what?" Beverly asked, but Hammer fell ent as he got an inkling of what Clint was planning.

127

"I think I know what you're getting at," Trap said and Hammer nodded.

"Will somebody tell me what he's getting at, then?" Beverly demanded.

"A stampede," Hammer said.

"What?" She was no longer disbelieving. She was now stunned. "Are you crazy?"

"It has to be done right, though," Hammer said.

"It's not hard to stampede a herd," Beverly said. "All they need is the slightest bit of provocation and they'll be long gone."

"What about stopping them?"

"*That's* the hard part," Beverly said.

"But it can be done?" Clint asked.

"If we had more men, but even with a full complement a herd is hell to stop once they get going." Frowning she asked, "Why the hell do you want to stampede my herd? We could end up back in Wyoming."

"Look, we don't even need a full scale stampede," Clint explained. "All I want them to do is walk very quickly . . . right through Granger's camp."

"Through his—wait a minute."

"Now she sees," Hammer said.

"If we run the herd through their camp they'll scatter to the four winds."

"And so will their horses," Trap pointed out.

"All right, let's examine this carefully," Clint said. "If we scatter them using the herd, they'll lose the time it takes them to round their horses up again."

"Right," Hammer said.

"And we stand to lose the time it might take us to round the herd up again."

"Right," Trap said.

"But we'll have our horses and they'll have to round their horses up on foot."

"Right," Beverly said.

"So even if both sides lose some time, they should lose more."

"Right," the Kid said.

"Sure, it all *sounds* right," Clint said, "but if we lose control of the herd it could take us forever just to stop them, and then we've got to get them turned around again."

"What if we don't use the whole herd?" Trap suggested.

"What do you mean?" Clint asked.

"We cut out maybe a quarter of the herd, we drive them around *behind* Granger's camp, and then run them through it. Now we've got them scattered, and we've got a quarter of the herd running in the right direction. When we get to here maybe the rest of the herd will stop them, or slow them down."

"That's good," Clint said, "but there's a better way."

"What's that?" Beverly asked.

"When that part of the herd reaches here we just get the rest of them running in the right direction, and then we let them run themselves out."

"By the time they do that, we'll have put a lot of distance between ourselves and Granger's scattered forces," Hammer added.

"Right."

They all sat in silence, considering the plan as they had all presented it.

"Okay," Beverly said. "I like it."

They all nodded their agreement.

"When do we do it?" Hammer asked.

"We can do it tonight," Clint said. "Hammer and I will ride back and find their camp while the rest of you cut out a quarter of the herd."

As they were all standing up Trap said, "Let's not miss something here."

"What's that?" Clint asked.

"Granger's got to have somebody watching us. If he sees us cutting out a quarter of the herd at night he's going to know something's happening."

"All right, then," Clint said, "you and the Kid find whoever he is and take care of him. Beverly, you and your men will have to cut the herd."

"Right."

"All right," Clint said, standing up, "we all know what we have to do."

"What if Granger's camped too far back?" Hammer asked, bringing up perhaps one last obstacle to the plan.

"He can't be too far behind," Clint said, "and even if he is, as long as we can get into position by daybreak we can take them by surprise while their horses are still picketed."

"I can't argue with it," Hammer said.

"Can anyone else?"

He waited until each person had considered and shook their heads to indicate that they could find no fault with the plan.

"Right," Clint said, "we all know what we have to do. I suggest we get to it."

TWENTY-FIVE

Trap and the Kid left camp first, drifting on their horses as if they were simply going out to take up their own watch.

This was the tricky part, then, on which the entire plan hinged. Once they got to the herd they were going to keep on riding. If the man or men who were watching them caught on to the fact that something was up, it could spell the end of the whole idea.

Trap and the Kid rode out to the herd very casually, and as they reached it just kept right on going. There was a quarter moon, which was to their benefit, because there was not that much light to give them away.

Once they were away from the herd their problem was finding the vantage point of whoever was watching them. They couldn't afford just to ride around aimlessly. The decision had been made to give them twenty minutes to find the man or men, and then Clint and Hammer would leave camp, assuming that they could do so unseen, and Beverly and her men would begin to cut the herd.

They paused for a moment to consider their next move, and then Trap pointed to a small ridge east of the camp. Neither man wanted to speak because sound travelled too well at night, so the Kid simply nodded that he agreed that was a likely place to set up if someone wanted to watch the camp.

They began to work their way over there.

Clint and Hammer had saddled their horses, and were waiting in the shadows near the chuck wagon.

An additional problem had presented itself to them after Trap and the Kid left camp, and they had taken care of it without delay.

The problem was Pete the cook. If he was working for Granger, and saw that something was happening this late at night, he could have made some kind of a ruckus to alert someone watching.

Instead, Pete the cook was tied up in the chuck wagon with Manny Jeffers standing watch over him.

Now they only had to wait five more minutes, and they'd be on their way.

Trap pointed and the Kid nodded.

They had him spotted.

They both dismounted and while Trap held the horses, making sure they made no noise, the Kid began to creep up behind the watcher.

There was just one man and no evidence that a second was near. The Kid moved as silently as a thought, moved up behind the man and had him by the throat before his prey realized what was happening.

The Kid did not have Trap's strength, but thinking of the two men whose throats had been cut he held the pressure on the man's throat until the man went totally limp—and then held it for a count of ten more.

He dropped the dead man to the ground and returned to where Trap was holding the horses.

Their part was done. Now they had to go and help cut the herd.

It was up to Clint and Hammer to find Granger's camp, now, to keep the plan in motion.

Clint looked at Hammer.

Hammer looked at his watch.

"It's time."

"It's *about* time!"

When Trap and the Kid got back into camp, Beverly and her men were already moving.

"Did they get away, okay?" Trap asked.

"Fine," Beverly said.

"Then let's get this herd cut," the Kid said.

Clint and Hammer rode in the same silence that Trap and the Kid had maintained.

They both had their guesses at just how far back Granger would keep his crew, and as it turned out it was Hammer whose guess was correct—but the distance, greater than Clint had surmised, was not beyond their reach.

The camp was lit by several fires and it was easy to see that it was spread out. Still, if they drove the cows right down the center they would scatter the men and go right on through the horses.

Clint signalled that he had seen enough and they both

returned to their horses and started back to their camp where, hopefully, a quarter of the herd would be ready to go.

When they returned to camp the only person in it was Manny Jeffers, still watching over Pete the cook.

"They're out there with the herd," he told them.

"And Pete?"

"Still inside, safe and sound."

"I don't hear anything," Hammer said.

Clint had to give Beverly and her men credit. He couldn't hear anything, either. He had expected to hear the cows as they approached camp, but here they were in camp and there was still no audible indication that they were cutting out a fourth of the herd.

"Hey, am I being left out of this?" Manny Jeffers wanted to know.

"You're not being left out," Clint told him. "You're playing an important part by watching over Pete."

"Why don't we just kill him so I can go along?"

"You want to kill him, Manny?" Clint said. "You've got a gun. Go ahead, kill him."

Jeffers stared at Clint for a few moments, then said, "Okay, I guess I'll watch him."

"Good man."

At that point Beverly came riding in on Lance.

"Everything is ready," she called out, and then clapped her hand over her mouth.

"It's okay, they're far enough away that they won't hear you, but can you continue to keep the cows this quiet?"

"We can try, Clint."

"Well, if we're going to try," he said, clapping Hammer on the shoulder, "let's go ahead and try now."

• • •

The rest of their plan would take hours to put into effect now. They had to drive the cows far enough east so that when they started north Granger and his men couldn't hear them.

Clint rode behind the smaller herd, watching as Beverly's men—more than enough to handle a herd *this* size—expertly drove the herd without the shouting, whistling and hoopla they used during the day. They had left a small crew behind to control the remainder of the herd until they could return.

Riding along with him were Hammer, Trap and the Kid, and Beverly. They maintained silence and all in all the only sounds to pierce the night were the occasional bleats of the cows—not enough at this distance to alert anyone.

When they had travelled far enough to the north they turned the herd and started south again, guided by Clint and Hammer so that they were heading directly for Granger's camp.

"When should we start running them, Mrs. Press?" one of the men rode back to ask.

Beverly looked at Clint who said, "Why not now? They might hear us approaching, and we might as well be on the run so they won't have time to react."

The man looked at Beverly, who nodded, and he rode back to the herd.

They started the herd moving faster from behind, crowding the last cows with their horses until they broke into a trot. Soon, the entire group of sixty-some cows were moving at an easy gait.

Clint and Hammer broke away and rode ahead, and when they were able to see Granger's campfires, they rode back to the herd.

"Let's get them running," Clint said to one of the hands, and this time they all got into the act—Clint, Hammer, Trap and the Kid, Beverly—all using their horses, reins, quirts, to get the herd moving faster.

The cows began to bleat loudly, but by this time it was too late, for they were fast approaching Granger's camp.

TWENTY-SIX

"You hear something?" Colin McKenzie asked Joe Cantey. They were lying side by side in their bedrolls and McKenzie had to shake him awake to ask him the question.

"What the—"

"Listen. Do you hear it?"

"Hear what?"

"Cows."

"The herd?" Cantey said, frowning.

"We should be too far away to be able to hear them," McKenzie said, frowning with his hand to the ground, "or to feel them, unless . . ."

He stood up and called out, "Granger!"

Granger, wrapped in his bedroll on the other side of the fire, rolled over and peered at McKenzie, annoyance plain on his face.

"What are you yelling about?"

"Cows!" McKenzie called out.

"What?" Granger said, throwing off his blanket.

By this time the sound of the cows was getting louder and they could even hear the thunder caused by their hooves striking the ground.

McKenzie looked around, wild-eyed, as Cantey stood up next to him. All over camp men were rolling out of their bedrolls, looking around in confusion.

"Jesus," McKenzie said, "stampede . . ."

Granger was looking around just as the cows suddenly entered the sphere of light thrown by the campfires.

"Stampede!" McKenzie shouted, and then all hell broke loose.

The cows cut right straight through the heart of Granger's camp and his men scattered, panic stricken. It was only natural that they would think that the *entire* herd was running through their camp, and their only thought was to escape with their lives.

As the cows thundered through several men fell beneath their hooves. The horses, smelling the panic in the air, began to react, rearing up from the rope picket line that was holding them. Eventually, they broke loose and scattered and some of Granger's men fell prey to *their* hooves, as well.

McKenzie and Cantey went in separate directions and lost track of each other. Each man also lost track of Granger.

The night was filled suddenly with the painful cries of the cows who had run through the campfires, stamping them out but being burned in the process.

Beverly Press' cowhands rode through with the herd,

flanking them on either side, no longer driving them silently. From behind the herd came Clint and company, riding hard to keep up. Clint looked around in search of Granger but the moonlight was dim and the campfires had been put out, so there was very little to see beyond shadows darting back and forth, running for cover.

The thing that surprised Clint was that there was no gunfire from Granger's camp, no retaliation whatsoever, but then he had never been faced with a stampede and did not realize the panic that men reacted with when they thought that two hundred and fifty cows were bearing down on them.

Suddenly, they were through the camp completely and Clint reined in and turned to look behind them. Hammer came up alongside of him.

"Did you catch any sign of Granger?" Clint asked.

"No, none, but it was hard to see once the cattle trampled out the campfires."

"If we're lucky he's been hammered into the ground by those cows."

"We could go back and look."

"And so will they, whoever's left. You want to go in there shooting?"

"Not me."

"Me neither. Let's get going. It'll be light soon and we have to catch up to the rest of the herd."

They took one last look into the darkness behind them and Hammer said, "I don't think we'll be bothered by them for a while."

"I hope you're right."

TWENTY-SEVEN

As the sun came up John Granger surveyed the damage that had been done to his camp. Standing alongside him were Joe Cantey and Colin McKenzie.

"How many men did we lose?"

"Five," Cantey said.

"Dead?"

"Trampled to death."

"It wasn't the whole herd," Granger said.

"No."

"There were enough of them to do the damage, though," McKenzie said. "How the hell did they get behind us?"

"I don't know," Granger said.

"Who was watching them?"

"Dokes, but I guess we can assume that he's dead, too," Granger said. "This was Adams' idea, it had to be.'' Granger's tone was almost one of admiration.

"Christ . . .'' McKenzie said, under his breath.

"All right, let's get organized,'' Granger said.

"To do what?'' McKenzie demanded. "It's all over.''

"Get the men and start chasing down the horses.''

"By the time we catch the horses on foot they'll be long gone,'' McKenzie argued.

Granger turned to him and said, "Just do it.''

McKenzie attempted to match stares with Granger but backed down quickly and went off to do as he was told.

Granger turned to Cantey and said, "When we get a couple of horses, use them to round up the rest. How many men do we have left?''

"We'll have to take a count.''

"Right, do it.''

"What about McKenzie?''

Granger thought a moment then said, "We're going to need his gun right now.''

"What are you planning?''

"We're going to run those bastards down and take care of them.''

"They have a good head start.''

Granger turned to face Cantey, who shied away from the look in the man's eyes.

"At this point I don't care if the herd gets through. I want Hammer, I want the lady, and most of all I want Clint Adams.''

"What about those other two?''

"They're for you and McKenzie. You take care of them, and then you can take care of McKenzie.''

"There's no bonus money if that herd gets through.''

"You have a point,'' Granger admitted, tugging on his calfskin gloves. "I guess if the herd does get through, we'll just have to take it back, won't we?"

It was daylight by the time the main section of the herd came into view. The skeleton crew that had been left behind had begun to move them along, and from behind came the stampeding sixty-odd cows which ran into the main body and started them running, as well.

The cowhands quickly flanked the entire herd, joined by Trap and the Kid, all trying to keep the herd from spreading out and getting completely out of hand.

Clint, Hammer and Beverly rode along behind the herd, watching intently and hoping that their plans would not backfire.

"How long can they keep running?" Clint asked Beverly.

"There's no way of knowing, Clint. If we had more men we might be able to stop them, but all we can do now is try to contain them."

"Maybe we should go back and try to pick off Granger and his men in the daylight," Hammer suggested.

"I don't think so, Fred. I think we'd better stay with the herd. It's going to take a while for Granger to take stock of his losses, round up his horses and decide what his next step should be."

"We've got a long way to go to Texas, though," Beverly pointed out.

"Well, if we get lucky," Clint said, indicating the accelerating herd, "maybe they'll run all the way to Texas."

TWENTY-EIGHT

The herd did not run quite all the way to Texas, but the run did carry them into New Mexico. Since they were driving the steers to a Texas town on the Gulf, it made sense to cross into New Mexico rather than travel by way of Kansas.

Eventually when the herd ran itself down Beverly Press' cowhands were able to get ahead of the herd, slow it down and successfully stop it.

"We'll have to give them a rest," Beverly told Clint when he protested.

"Granger's going to be coming after us hard, Beverly," he explained. "Let's make this a short rest. Walking should be enough of a rest for them after all the running the poor beasts have done."

During the stop the hands switched horses, leaving their tired mounts in the hands of Manny Jeffers, who no longer had Pete the cook to look after.

During the stop Clint decided it was time to unload old Pete, and met with no resistance from anyone on the decision.

"You can't just leave me here," Pete protested.

"Your friends should be along soon, Pete," Clint told him. "I'm sure they'll give you a horse."

"Granger will leave me out here to rot!"

"If that's the case, I'd start walking if I was you. It shouldn't take you more than a couple of days to come to a town."

Clint would have preferred to leave the chuck wagon behind, as well, but Beverly protested, with good reason.

"We've still got a long way to go, and these men aren't going to be able to work if they don't eat. Also, their meals are part of their routine. Break the routine and they might not function as well."

They discussed using pack horses instead of the wagon, but that would have slowed them down even more than the chuckwagon did.

"All right," Hammer said after all those problems had been resolved, "now who's going to do the cooking?"

Clint, Hammer, Trap and the Kid all looked at Beverly who said, "Wait a minute. I know I'm the only woman on this drive, but let's not lose sight of the fact that I'm also the boss lady."

"Yeah, and I've tasted her cooking before," Clint informed them.

"What's wrong with my—" she started to retort, but then realized what Clint was trying to do. "Oh no, you're not going to get me that way. We five are going to share the cooking—"

"But—" Hammer started.

"And if you don't agree," she went on, charging right past his objection, "you don't eat."

"Okay," Hammer said, "but I'm warning you, Pete is going to start looking good every fifth day."

"Well," Clint said, looking at the others, "how much worse can *we* be than Pete was?"

"Speak for yourself," Trap said. "I happen to be a real good cook."

"Good," Beverly said, "so you can start us off tonight—and if you're real good, maybe I'll hire you permanently."

"That's fine with me," he said, "but you'll have to pay me a lot more than you are now!"

By the time Granger had picked up the pieces of his camp and crew, he had fifteen men left, twelve horses, and limited supplies.

"Can we make up a full day on them?" Cantey asked.

"It depends on whether or not they were able to stop the herd," Granger said.

Some of his men were still out trying to find three more horses.

"What about the amount of men we have left?" Cantey asked. "Our force has been cut in half."

"They've been lucky up to now," Granger said, "but their luck has run out."

"McKenzie's complaining that we don't have such a manpower advantage, anymore."

"McKenzie's making it hard for me to keep him alive," Granger said. "Look, we've got fifteen gun-hands, while if they have fifteen men at all two-thirds of them are cowhands and plough boys. The only guns we have to worry about are Clint Adams' and Fred Hammer's. You're going to take care of Hammer while I handle the Gunsmith." Granger looked at Cantey and said, "You can take care of that big black bastard, can't you?"

"No problem."

Granger stared off in the direction that the stampeding herd had taken and said, "We'll stay right here for the night, Cantey. Let them have their full day's head start. Let them think that they got the better of me, because they're in for a big surprise."

"Do you intend to stop off in a town for more supplies?"

"Hell, no," Granger said. "That's one advantage of having lost so many men, isn't it?"

"What is?"

"We're not as short on supplies as we might have been."

"You're hired," Beverly Press told Trap later that evening. "That was delicious."

"It's the same stew Pete made many times," Trap said modestly.

"That may be," Beverly said, "but his never tasted like yours."

"You were telling the truth, Trap," Clint said. "You can cook."

"Have I ever lied to you?"

"We can discuss that after I come off my watch," Clint said, standing up.

Hammer put down his empty plate and also stood to accompany Clint. They had agreed that two man watches would be enough, giving the rest of the men time to rest. It was virtually impossible that Granger and his men would catch up to them that night.

The next night, however, they'd go back to the triple watches.

Out on watch Clint and Hammer could hear the heavy breathing of the herd.

"Did we lose any steers?" Clint asked.

"Five or six dropped dead during the run, but they probably wouldn't have lasted the trip, anyway."

"You an expert on cows, now?"

"Actually, they're steers—but no. One of Mrs. Press' men told me that."

"Well, I hope the others are recovered by tomorrow," Clint said.

"Not to mention the horses."

"Running comes a lot more naturally to horses than steers." Actually, that was just his opinion, but it sounded good. "They should be fine. As for the cattle, we can walk them for a while and give them some additional rest that way."

"How long do you think it will take Granger to regroup his crew?"

"I figure we've got a day's head start minimum—that is, if Granger himself wasn't injured. If that's the case, we may be home free."

"Somehow, I doubt that," Hammer said. "Granger was probably the first one out of camp when we drove the cattle through."

"Yeah," Clint said. "I doubt that we caught him as flatfooted as we would have liked."

After a few moments of silence Hammer said, "You know, this could set a madman like Granger off."

"Is he mad?"

"Stark raving. Oh, he keeps it under control, but after what we did to him—what *you* did to him—he's going to be on a pretty short fuse."

"He'll still want to face me head on."

"For your rep?"

Clint nodded.

"Anybody who'd wear calfskin gloves and go by the name 'Tenderhands'—"

"Like you go by the name 'the Gunsmith?' "

"No, I think it's by choice with him, otherwise he could have done away with the gloves . . . *and* the name."

"And in order to get rid of your name, you'd have to get rid of your gun."

"Exactly."

"Which would be like committing suicide."

Clint nodded.

"And I'm not ready to go to those lengths, not even to do away with the name 'Gunsmith.' "

TWENTY-NINE

For the rest of the drive Clint had at least one man ride well behind the herd, keeping watch for Granger and his men. They couldn't drive the herd as hard as he would have liked for fear of losing too many more along the way, so he wanted to make sure that he knew if Granger and his crew had been able to make up the full day lead they had on him.

"What are we going to do if they start to gain on us?" Beverly had asked him.

"I don't know," he replied. "We'll just have to wait and see if it happens."

They were in Texas, about four days from their destination, when Trap, who was on lookout, spotted the dust cloud a couple of miles off. From the size of it he guessed there were at least a dozen riders, coming hard.

151

He wheeled his horse around and rode hell-bent for leather back to the herd.

"These horses ain't gonna stand up to this for too much longer," McKenzie said to Granger.

They had stopped just to give the horses a short blow, and McKenzie's words were the last thing Granger needed at that moment.

They were both mounted and Granger swung his right hand backhanded, catching McKenzie flush on the face. The force of the blow knocked him from the saddle and he landed on the ground with a painful thud.

"What the fuck—" he said.

Cantey had seen the blow coming and was prepared to act if McKenzie were to try and draw on Granger.

McKenzie's hand actually started for his gun reflexively, but he quickly realized that drawing on Granger would be committing suicide.

"What the hell was that for?" he demanded instead, glaring up at Granger.

"You've done nothing but bitch and moan since we started out, and I'm tired of it," Granger said wearily. "It's my guess that we're no more than a couple of hours behind the herd now, but if that's not good enough for you then you'd better keep your mouth shut. In fact, I want you to keep it shut for the rest of this trip, understand?"

"Now wait a minute—"

Granger drew his gun and pointed it at McKenzie, who stopped talking and swallowed hard. There was a mad glint in Granger's eyes, and he thought for sure that he was about to be killed.

Cantey watched, holding his breath, waiting for Granger to shoot. The man with the gloves had drawn his gun faster than anyone Cantey had ever seen, and he too thought that McKenzie was as good as dead.

"I need your gun, McKenzie," Granger said, "not your mouth. What do you say?"

"S-sure, Granger, fine," McKenzie stammered. "Whatever you say."

"Remember that," Granger said, holstering his gun almost as fast as he'd drawn it, "the next time you think of something to complain about."

McKenzie closed his eyes and leaned back on his hands, his body flooded first with relief, and then suddenly with anger. He opened his eyes and looked up at Granger's back, which had invitingly been turned to him.

All it would take was one shot, he thought.

Cantey watched McKenzie carefully, because he knew that if Granger had shamed him that way and then turned his back on him, he would have shot him in the back. However, he couldn't afford to have McKenzie do that, so he was prepared to kill the man on the ground if he made a move for his gun.

He didn't. He obviously thought better of the move and simply climbed to his feet.

"Let's get going," Granger said, and started his horse forward. The other men, who had simply been milling about, moved behind Granger, followed by Cantey and finally, Colin McKenzie.

When Trap reached the herd he quickly found Clint and reported what he'd seen.

"Did you see how many?"

"I didn't want to wait that long," Trap said, "but from the size of the dust cloud they were kicking up I'd say there were at least a dozen."

"We'd match up pretty good with them now," Hammer offered.

"If we were just dealing with numbers we would," Clint agreed, "but we've got cowhands and Granger has gunhands—second-raters, but still gunhands."

"What's wrong?" Beverly asked, riding over.

"They're catching up," Clint said.

"What do we do?"

"We're going to have to stop them in their tracks for a while, until we can build up a big lead again."

"How do you propose to do that?" Trap asked.

Clint thought a moment, then made his decision.

"Two men with rifles," he said, "could hold them off for a while if they had a good vantage point." He looked at Trap and asked, "What about it? Did you see a spot?"

Trap thought a moment and while he was thinking the Kid came riding abreast of them.

"There is a spot," Trap said. "It's just a stand of trees, but it would hide two men all right—but no more."

"We won't need more," Clint said, looking at Hammer. "What do you say, Fred?"

"Let us do it," Trap said. "You and Hammer keep driving the herd. We'll keep them off your back for a good long while."

"Can you catch up afterwards?" Beverly asked.

"If we can, they can," Trap said. Looking at Clint he said, "I think we should pin them down, run ahead of them, wait for them to catch up and pin them down again, and then repeat the sequence."

"For how long?" Clint asked.

"Until the herd reaches its destination," Trap said.

"Why you?" Clint asked.

"The herd needs you," Trap said. "Besides, you've seen the Kid handle a gun—*and* we're pretty damn tired of eating dust."

Clint didn't believe the last bit, but the rest of it made sense.

"You're going to need plenty of ammunition, and a lot of beef jerky," he said. "Any more supplies than that would slow you down."

"Makes sense," the Kid said. "Let's get outfitted, Trap. I'd rather do this than drive cows, anyway."

"Right."

When they left Hammer looked at Clint and asked, "Are they going to stall them, or pick them off?"

"I guess whatever the situation allows," Clint said. "It doesn't really matter as long as they keep them off our backs for the next four days."

"That's a lot to ask of them," Beverly said.

"We didn't ask," Clint said. "Besides I think the Kid was telling the truth. They'd rather that than driving cattle." Clint stretched in the saddle and added, "I can't say as I wouldn't prefer it, myself."

THIRTY

It was coming up on two hours that Trap and the Kid had been waiting for Granger and his men to show up, and much of that time had been spent in silence. The two young men had been friends long enough that they didn't feel the need to fill every moment with chatter. One usually knew what the other was thinking, anyway.

And then, sometimes, they just needed to talk.

"Kid?"

"Yeah, Trap."

"Why are we doing this?"

"What?"

"All of this," the Kid said, spreading his hands expansively, "but especially this."

"You mean waiting here in a clump of trees for twelve to fifteen men to come along so *we* can start shooting at *them*?"

"That's what I mean."

"We're just the helpful types, I guess."

"I know that, but in the past we've always been helpful to *ourselves*. In fact you might say that we've always helped ourselves," the Kid added, thinking of a bank and train or two.

"I know what you mean."

"So what changed us?"

Trap made a show of considering the question before answering.

"We like cows?"

"They're not cows, they're steers, and no, we don't like them."

"How about Mrs. Press? We both like her?"

"She's an attractive woman, no question about that, but let's face it she's too old for either of us."

"Speak for yourself," Trap (who was three months older than his friend) said, "I happen to like older women."

"And she's only got eyes for Clint Adams."

"The Gunsmith," Trap said, making the name sound almost like a benediction.

"Ri-i-ight," the Kid agreed, drawing it out.

They lapsed in a momentary silence, and then Trap said, "That's it, isn't it?"

"What is, Trap?"

"The Gunsmith. He's the real reason we're going through all this."

"Yeah, I guess he is," the Kid agreed, "but the man is a legend, you know."

"And *he's* impressed with *you*," Trap said, poking the Kid in the chest playfully.

"And curious about us both."

"True."

"Too true."

"So why are we doing this?" It was the Kid asking the question, this time.

"Maybe because he bailed us out of jail . . ."

"Right."

". . . or because he asked us to . . ."

"Right."

". . . or maybe it's because it will be something to tell our grandchildren when we get older, that we worked with 'the Gunsmith.' "

"Yeah, right," Trap said, "grandchildren."

"Yeah."

"Kid?"

"Yeah?"

Trap turned to look at his friend and the Kid knew a serious question was coming.

"Could you take him?"

"Shit, I don't know," the Kid said, without hesitation. He had thought about it, but had been able to come to no clear cut conclusion.

"I told him you could."

"Well, thanks," the Kid said sarcastically. "I hope he doesn't decide that *he'd* like to find out."

"You don't think you can take him, do you?"

"I told you, I don't know."

"Do you know how fast you are, Kid?"

"I'm faster than most," the Kid said with a shrug.

"You're the fastest there is."

"So you keep telling me."

"*I* believe it."

"I appreciate your faith, Trap, I really do, but do me a favor?"

"What?"

"Don't keep braggin' about me, not to the Gunsmith."

"How about to Mrs. Press? And Hammer?"

"Nobody. Let's just keep our heads down, get this job done, have our little piece of history, and get a move on. What do you say?"

Trap straightened up and, peering straight ahead, said, "I say, I see a dust cloud."

"Well, it's about time," the Kid said in mock relief. "I thought for sure you were going to talk me to death before they could get here to kill me."

Granger was riding in front with a man on either side. Just behind him was Cantey, and bringing up the rear was McKenzie, who was still feeling shame from Granger's treatment.

The first shot took the man on Granger's right out of the saddle, and the second shot punched a hole in the shoulder of the man on the left.

Granger did not shout to his men to take cover as he scrambled from the saddle, because if they were too stupid to do so without having to be told, then they deserved to die.

"Trap, I keep telling you that rifle of yours pulls to the left," the Kid scolded his friend. "You should have taken that man right out of his saddle."

"Well, excuse me for not being Mr. Perfect Aim, like you."

"And I've told you before you don't aim a gun, you *point* it, as if it was your finger."

"Why don't you shut up, point your finger out there and fire a few more shots. We're supposed to be keeping them pinned down, remember?"

"Jeez," the Kid said, firing a couple of shots quickly. "Try to help a guy out . . ."

•   •   •

"What's going on?" Cantey asked.

He, Granger and the others had sought cover wherever they could, lying behind rocks and stones, in depressions in the ground, or simply lying as flat as they possibly could.

Granger and Cantey had found refuge in the same depression, and were lying side by side.

"Adams," Granger said.

"He's out there?"

"Maybe," Granger said, "or he may have just left some men behind. The point is, they're supposed to keep us pinned down as long as they can, giving the herd time to get further away."

"And our bonus gets further aways, too."

"Maybe not," Granger said. "Start firing—"

"We don't even know where they are."

"They're in that stand of trees, Cantey."

"Our handguns won't reach that far," Cantey said. "They're obviously using rifles."

Most of the men had scrambled out of their saddles, leaving their rifles behind. Granger, Cantey and McKenzie had taken theirs by reflex.

"You and McKenzie might be able to do some damage, and I'll pass my rifle over to one of the men. The others can just make some noise."

"What's the purpose?"

"To cover me," Granger said. "I'm going to catch up with that herd."

"This is getting boring," the Kid said, reloading.

"What the—What's he doing?"

The Kid looked up and saw what Trap meant. One man had risen and was running in a crouch toward the nearest horse.

"Who is that?" the Kid asked.

"I can't say for sure, but I'd bet it's Granger."

"We'd better stop him."

They both got ready to fire when suddenly a barrage of bullets bit into the trees around them.

"Jesus," the Kid said, ducking back, "I thought they all left their rifles behind."

"Reflexes," the Kid said. "Granger and a couple of the others probably grabbed theirs by reflex." When the firing continued the Kid said, "Yeah, I'd guess three rifles. The rest of the shooting is just for effect."

"Yeah, well, the effect is that Granger's getting away."

"What can he do," the Kid asked, "stampede the herd by himself?"

It got quiet suddenly and they exchanged a glance.

"We'd better get to the horses."

As they began to stand up straight the firing started again and they ducked back down.

"He's going to get ahead of us," the Kid said.

"They're the ones who are pinned down, Kid, not us."

"Let's back out of here."

They had left their horses out behind the clump of trees and now they backed up until they were clear of any firing, then scrambled out to where their horses were and mounted up.

"This whole thing is going to backfire on us," Trap said as they mounted up.

"Why do you say that?"

"While we're chasing him," Trap said, jerking his head behind him to indicate Granger's men, "they're going to be chasing us!"

THIRTY-ONE

"How do you think Trap and the Kid are doing?"
Hammer asked Clint.

"It's been two days," Clint said. "Hopefully, they've
delayed Granger and his men long enough for us to get
this beef delivered."

"Hopefully," Hammer said.

They were only two days away from their destination
and they could all smell the end of the trail after a long,
hard drive.

"I don't think I'll ever do this again," Clint said.

"I don't think I will, either," Beverly said, coming up
alongside of him.

"Me, neither," Hammer said.

"Still," Clint said, "it has been an experience . . ."

"Well," the Kid said, "at least it's not boring, anymore."

They had stopped to give their horses a rest, although they couldn't give the animals the rest they deserved.

They had spent the past day trying to catch up to Granger while trying to stay ahead of his men. Every so often, when they felt his men breathing down their neck, they'd stop, seek cover and pin them down again, and then jump on their horses and take advantage of a small head start. Unfortunately, every time they had to stop they got further behind Granger.

"He's going to reach the herd before we can get him," Trap said. "If he does, then we'll have failed to do our job."

"Maybe the herd will get delivered before he gets there," the Kid said, "which means we *will* have done our job."

"Yeah," Trap said, doubtfully. "We'd better get a move on or we'll have to stop again."

They mounted up and checked behind them. A cloud of dust was closing fast.

"Let's ride!" Trap said.

"That's it," Beverly Press said, "Southport."

"Where does the herd go?"

"There's a ranch about two miles beyond. We've got to go around the town."

"Where is this ranch, in the water?"

They were so close to the ocean that they could smell it.

"My friend runs his cattle about fifty miles north of here," she explained. "He had to drive his here for the pickup, as well."

"I hope we got here in time."

"We did," she said. "There will be three pickups, and we should be here in time for the second."

"Well, let's get them moving, then."

They were ahead of the herd, checking on how close they were to town. As they turned their horses to return Beverly put her hand on Clint's arm.

"Clint, before we go back to the herd I want to tell you how much I appreciate what you've done."

"There's no need to thank me, Beverly."

"Not with words, maybe," she said, "but after we deliver the herd, I'm going to thank you properly."

"Like I said, then," Clint said, "let's get them moving."

They rode back to the herd and Clint said to Hammer, "We can see the town, which means we've got two miles to go."

"Jesus," Hammer said; "I thought we'd never get there."

"And all in once piece, too," Beverly said.

Before she could laugh the bullet struck her high on the left side, knocking her right out of the saddle, and the echo of the shot came seconds later.

Clint and Hammer were off their horses quickly, Clint leaning over Beverly and Hammer searching for where the shot came from.

"Spot him?" Clint asked, trying to stop the bleeding of Beverly's wound.

"No," Hammer said, "and he won't fire again because he'd give his location away."

"Granger?"

"That'd be my guess. Somehow, he got past Trap and the Kid."

Neither of them voiced the possibility that he might not only have gotten past them, but killed them, too.

"How bad?" Hammer asked.

"I can't be sure," Clint said, packing the wound.

"I'm going to have to get her into town to a doctor, Hammer," he looked up at the black man and said, "Can you take the herd on ahead?"

"You bet."

"She said there's a ranch two miles beyond town."

"We'll find it. You take care of her."

Beverly was semi-conscious, a look of pain on her face. She opened her eyes and said, "Clint—"

"Easy, Bev," Clint said. "You're going to be fine."

"The herd."

"They'll be fine, too." Clint looked at Hammer and said, "I'll need one man, you take the rest."

Hammer helped Clint get Beverly up onto her horse and then the two men faced each other.

"Get this herd delivered," Clint said. "When you get them bedded down, meet me at the saloon."

"Right. My guess is Granger's alone, Clint," Hammer said, "and that's when he's the most dangerous. Watch yourself."

"He's the one who has to watch himself," Clint said. "He ambushed a woman, and when the herd is delivered, I'm going to find him, Hammer. I'll find him and show him what a mistake that was."

THIRTY-TWO

Clint Adams was sitting in a chair on the boardwalk outside the doctor's office when Trap and the Kid came riding in, looking completely beat. Trap spotted him, nudged the Kid and they rode over.

"Clint," Trap said.

"What happened?"

"Granger got by us," Trap said, and went on to explain how they got stuck between chasing him down and staying ahead of his crew.

It was the Kid who noticed that they were in front of a doctor's office and he asked, "What happened here, Clint?"

"Granger caught up to us enough to take a shot at us."

"Who got hit?"

"Beverly Press."

"Oh, no," Trap said.

"It's our fault," the Kid said.

"It's nobody's fault," Clint said, "except for Granger."

"Is she—how is she?" Trap asked.

"The doctor's looking at her now. The shot took her high up on the left side. What happened to Granger's men?"

"They've probably joined him outside of town," Trap said. "Where's the herd?"

"Hammer took it on ahead while I brought Beverly to the doc."

"Are we in the clear, then?" the Kid asked, but at that moment the door to the doctor's office opened and a man stepped out. He was a tall, slender man in his mid-forties and the sign next to his door said his name was Doctor E.J. Bookman.

"Doc?" Clint said, standing up.

"She was very lucky," the doctor said. "A little lower and the bullet would have nicked her heart. She'll be all right, but she's going to need a lot of rest."

"Can I see her?"

"Sure, but just for a minute."

"Put your horses up in the livery, fellas, and then meet me at the saloon," Clint told Trap and the Kid.

"Clint, we're sorry—"

"Don't apologize," Clint said, cutting him off, "just meet me in the saloon."

They watched him go into the doctor's office and then started walking their horses to the livery.

Inside the doctor showed Clint into his examining room, where Beverly Press was lying on a table, covered with a white sheet that almost matched the pallor of her face.

"Beverly . . ."

Her eyes fluttered open and she smiled wanly at him.

"How are you doing?" he asked her.

"I feel a little weak, but otherwise I'm fine. How's the herd?"

"Hammer took it on ahead. By now they should be safe and sound with your friend."

"Then we made it?"

"Sure," he said, giving her hand a squeeze, "we made it."

"That's all, please," the doctor said from behind.

Clint kissed her lightly on the lips and said, "I'll back later. I'm going to get you a room at the hotel."

She nodded, no energy to argue even if she wanted to.

As Clint followed the doctor outside the man said, "Our sheriff would like you to stop by his office and have a talk with him."

"I will."

"I, uh, think he wanted you to do it right away."

"I've got to talk to my two friends first, but I'll check in with him right after."

"Okay." The doctor's tone said that he delivered his message and it was up to Clint to do the rest.

"By the way," Clint said from the door, "what's the sheriff's name?"

"Barker, Sheriff Dan Barker."

"Okay. Thanks, Doc. What do I owe you?"

"You can pay me when you come back for her."

"I'll be by for her later—right after I see the sheriff."

Trap and the Kid were waiting in the saloon when Clint entered. They had already taken a back table and were working on two beers. Clint got a beer from the bartender and joined them, taking the seat they had left him, against the wall.

Trap bit back the urge to apologize again and waited for Clint to speak.

"I want Granger," he said.

"For shooting Mrs. Press?" Trap asked.

Clint nodded.

"You don't think he was aiming for you?"

"If he was I wouldn't be here. No, he wanted me to be mad enough to go after him."

"We'll help you," Trap said immediately, and the Kid nodded his agreement.

"Not with Granger," Clint said, "but I might need you for the others."

"Do you think he'll go after the herd after its been delivered?" Trap asked.

"No. Beverly's friend has enough hands with him to make that a dumb move, but Granger's not going to like it that we kept him from doing his job. I'm sure he was promised a bonus, and now he won't get it."

"So then you won't have to go after him," the Kid said, "he'll come after you."

"Probably, but if he rides into town it won't be alone."

"He'll face you alone, though," the Kid said. "He'd want to do it that way because of who you are."

"That's what I'd think," Clint said, "but I never would have guessed him for a man who would bush-wack a woman. He's too unpredictable after that."

"We'll stand with you, Clint."

"I appreciate it," Clint said, "but don't do it out of any false sense of guilt."

"We're not," Trap said.

"We're doing it because we want something to tell our grandchildren."

•   •   •

"The men want to head back," Cantey said.

"What about the rest?"

"They'll ride into town with you," Cantey said, "if you'll pay them."

"Let them go, then," Granger said. He turned to face Cantey and said, "What about you? You want to be paid?"

"It wouldn't hurt."

"I wouldn't need you for the Gunsmith," Granger said. "I'll take care of him myself. It's the others, Hammer, and those other two. If they're with him—"

"He'll face you alone," Cantey said.

"Yeah, he will," Granger said. "I've made sure of that."

"You want McKenzie, too?"

Granger made a face and said, "He's a decent gun-hand, so I guess we better take him. Cut the rest loose."

"Right."

Granger sat astride his fort looking down at the town of Southport. Clint Adams was waiting for him there, he was sure, and he wasn't going to keep him waiting long.

After all, the Gunsmith owed him money, the money he would have been paid by Crandall for stopping the herd.

It never once occurred to Granger that his failure might have been his own fault for mishandling the entire affair.

It was all Clint Adams' fault.

THIRTY-THREE

Clint looked past Trap and the Kid at the man who entered the saloon and saw the badge on his shirt.

"You fellas have any reason that you might not want to talk to the law?"

They resisted the urge to turn around, and Clint could see by the look on their faces that talking with lawmen was not their favorite pastime.

"All right, why don't you take your beers and move to another table, and don't make a big production about it."

The two of them picked up their beers and casually moved two tables away. The sheriff watched them without interest, then approached Clint.

"Are you the man who brought the wounded woman in?"

"That's me."

"Didn't you get my message from the doc?"

"You must be Sheriff Barker."

"That's right."

Barker was a big, barrel-chested man with a solid chin and high forehead. His receding hair was slate grey and curled tightly to his head.

"What's your name?"

"Adams, Clint Adams."

He could see that the man recognized the name.

"Well, Mr. Adams, do you want to tell me what happened?"

"Somebody shot Mrs. Press, the lady I work for."

"Doing what?"

"We drove a herd past your town this morning. I'm the ramrod."

"I see. Any idea who did it?"

"None."

"Where'd you drive the herd from?"

"Wyoming."

"You have any trouble along the trail?"

"Nope."

"So why would somebody want to shoot your boss?"

Clint shrugged.

"Maybe you should ask her."

"Maybe I will."

"I'll tell her you're coming, as soon as I get her settled into the hotel."

"I don't want any trouble in this town, Adams," the sheriff said, pointing his finger.

"I don't blame you, Sheriff," Clint said. "It seems like a nice, quiet town."

"And I want it kept that way." He looked over at Trap and the Kid and asked, "Are those two with you?"

"We were just trying to get up a poker game. Maybe

when it gets a little later in the day we'll find another couple of players to fill a table."

"How long you planning on staying in town?"

"Until my boss is ready to ride."

"I'll have my eye on you."

"I appreciate that, Sheriff."

The lawman glared at Clint for a few moments, then turned and stalked out. Trap and the Kid picked up their beers and returned to the table.

"Why don't one of you see if you can't get a deck of cards from the bartender," Clint said. "If the sheriff comes back we should look like we're playing poker."

He started to rise and Trap said, "Where are you going?"

"I'm going to get Beverly settled in the hotel, and then I'll be back. We might as well wait right here for Hammer to get back."

"Or for Granger to get here."

"Him, too."

Clint virtually carried Beverly from the doctor's office to the hotel and got her settled in her room.

"Have we gotten virtuous suddenly?" she asked, referring to the fact that they were not sharing a room.

"You can do without bouncing around in bed for a while," he told her. "I'll be right next door."

She was more lucid than she had been, and proved it with her next question.

"You figure it was Granger who shot me?"

"Yup."

"Why?"

"We beat him," Clint said. "He doesn't like that. He wanted to make sure I was mad enough to face him when he rode in."

"Don't."

"What?" He was deliberately being dense.

"Don't face him, not on my account."

"I may not have any choice, Beverly. Granger's wanted me from the beginning. It's the nature of the beast."

"What beast?"

"The kind of beast Granger is," he explained, "a predator."

"A killer."

"That, too," Clint said, and then added, "but a lot of people put me in the same class."

"They don't know you."

He smiled and said, "Not like you do." He leaned over and kissed her.

"Where are you going?"

"To the saloon. I think I've earned a few drinks, don't you?"

She nodded and said, "And more—which I will show you after I've healed. I had no idea it was such an inconvenience to get shot."

"I've never heard it described that way before," he said, "but I guess you're right." He walked to the door and said, "Get some rest and whatever you do, don't try to get out of that bed. I shouldn't be gone long."

"No," she said as he left and closed the door, "just long enough to kill—or get killed."

THIRTY-FOUR

Clint was crossing the street to the saloon when he saw Hammer riding into town from the south. He turned and went to meet him.

"Everything okay?" he asked.

"The herd is delivered. Mrs. Press' friend is concerned about her and said he'd be in after he checked out the herd."

"We in time for the pickup?"

"Three days."

"Good."

"Trap and the Kid show up?"

"Yeah. Granger just got by them."

Hammer shrugged.

"It happens."

"How is Mrs. Press?"

"She'll be fine. She's at the hotel, resting."

"That's good."

"Put your horse up and join us in the saloon."

"I've been dreaming about a drink for miles. Be right with you."

They parted company, Hammer heading for the livery and Clint for the saloon.

Hammer was still dreaming of a drink when he entered the livery. There was no liveryman in evidence so he went ahead and picked out a stall and began to remove the saddle from his horse himself.

"Hello, Hammer," he heard a voice say from behind. Instinct told him there was a gun on him and he froze.

"Hello, Granger."

"You chose the wrong side, Hammer."

Hammer shrugged his big shoulders and said, "The herd got delivered."

"Undo your gunbelt."

Hammer briefly considered making some kind of move but changed his mind when he was flanked by two men: Cantey and McKenzie.

"I'll help you," Cantey said.

"Hello, Joe," Hammer said as the man reached across him to unbuckle his belt for him. McKenzie stood nearby with his gun out. "It's nice to see a friendly face."

"You ain't no friend of mine, Hammer," Cantey said, moving away with the gunbelt.

"You can turn around now, Hammer."

The big black man turned around and faced Granger, who was tugging on the end of his gloves.

"What now?"

"Grab a seat somewhere and sit tight. McKenzie, you have a message to deliver. Get it done."

"A message?"

"To your friend the Gunsmith. If he wants to see you in one piece again he'll be over here soon."

"You want to face the Gunsmith?" Hammer asked, his voice thick with disdain.

"I'm going to kill him."

"It's going to take more than a couple of silly looking gloves to kill—" Hammer started, but he stopped short when Granger took two steps and drove a gloved fist into the black man's face. Hammer took the blow well, taking one step back and retaining his balance.

"Get moving, McKenzie!" Granger snapped.

Hammer licked some blood from his split lip and said to Granger, "I owe you one."

Clint had bought a beer for Hammer, anticipating his arrival, and was starting to think it was going to get warm when the batwing doors opened.

The man who entered was not Hammer. Clint recognized him as one of the men he had seen on the porch during his first visit to Crandall's ranch.

"Watch it," Clint said to Trap and the Kid.

The man stood just inside the doorway, looking around. A few more customers had come in since they had first entered the saloon, and the man was obviously looking around for someone. When his eyes fell on Clint's table he began to walk tentatively toward it.

"Adams."

"What can I do for you?"

"My name's McKenzie—"

"Never heard of you."

That stopped him momentarily, but then he surged on.

"I have a message for you."

"From who?"

"Granger."

"Deliver it."

"He's got your friend Hammer over at the livery stable. He says if you want to see him alive again you'll head right over there."

"He's got Hammer," the Kid said, "and we've got you."

McKenzie looked wary, as if he wanted to run but thought they might shoot him down if he did.

"No good," Clint said. McKenzie looked at him as if he were his savior.

"Clint—" the Kid said.

"It's hardly what I'd call an even trade, Hammer for this piece of shit." Clint directed his attention to McKenzie and said, "You tell Granger I'll be over directly."

McKenzie sent a nervous glance the Kid's way and said, "Alone."

"I don't need any help with Granger," Clint said. "You tell him I said that."

"I'll tell him."

"Then move."

Again McKenzie looked at Trap and the Kid nervously, then started to back away towards the batwing doors. The Kid considered jumping up from his seat all of a sudden, seeing just how much he could scare the man, but it wasn't time for games like that, not with Hammer's life on the line.

After McKenzie left Clint finished his beer and then drank some of Hammer's.

"We're going with you," Trap said, as if he expected Clint to argue.

"Damn right, you are."

THIRTY-FIVE

It was close to dark when McKenzie delivered the message to Clint, and the Gunsmith deliberately waited for darkness to fall before he left the saloon. He very briefly considered going for the sheriff, but was never serious about it. All that would probably do was get the lawman killed.

He walked down the boardwalk of the main street toward the livery and as he approached the bar stepped out into the center of the street.

The livery stable doors opened at that point and Hammer stepped out. His hands were behind his back and it was obvious that his hands were tied.

"Hey, Hammer," Clint called.

"Bad situation, huh?" Hammer asked.

"Could be worse."

"How?"

"It could be my life that depended on you."

At that point Granger came out from the dark interior of the livery and stood next to Hammer.

"From where I stand you're holding your own life in your hands, Adams."

"I wouldn't have it any other way, Granger. Why don't you just step away from Hammer."

"Not yet."

Granger put his hand against Hammer's chest and shoved the big black man backward. Hammer's progress was stopped abruptly when McKenzie stepped out and caught him, putting his gun to his head.

"What's that for, Granger?" Clint demanded. "I thought this was between you and me."

Granger grinned and said, "Insurance."

"Where's Cantey?"

"More insurance."

"How do I know I'm not in for a bullet in the back?"

"I don't need to have someone backshoot you, Adams. I can outdraw you."

"Not on the best day you ever had, Granger."

They faced each other then, Tenderhands against the Gunsmith, with Tenderhands holding the edge in the person of Fred Hammer.

McKenzie kept the barrel of his gun pressed up against Hammer's neck. He had orders to shoot at the first sign of trouble. He wondered idly if that meant that Granger had his doubts about whether or not he could take the Gunsmith.

McKenzie's hand was sweating and he flexed it on the butt of his gun.

"You getting nervous, McKenzie?"

"Shut up."

"It's real dark in here, McKenzie, you sure we're alone?"

"What are you talking about?"

"Maybe he's talking about this," a voice said from behind him.

McKenzie felt the barrel of a gun pressed against his neck and heard the sound of the hammer being cocked.

"Take your gun away from his neck," Trap said into McKenzie's ear.

"I'll shoot."

"Fine, and then I'll shoot you. If that's an even trade in your mind, go ahead."

As far as McKenzie was concerned, nothing was an even trade for his life. He lowered his gun and it was taken from his hand.

"Okay, now let's just watch."

It was extremely hard for the Kid to get up onto the roof of the livery without making noise, but he managed to accomplish it with a *minimum* of noise.

Trap and the Kid had left the saloon ahead of Clint Adams, had located both Cantey and McKenzie and got into position to take care of them to keep them from interfering in the confrontation between Clint Adams and Granger.

Cantey was on the roof, lying on his belly overlooking the front of the livery, where Granger had told him to position himself. He became aware that someone was behind him but by the time he rolled over to take a look the Kid was almost on him, gun in hand.

"Just roll right back over, Cantey, and watch carefully," the Kid said.

Cantey briefly considered going for his gun, but was not in a position to do so with any authority. Meekly, he rolled back over onto his belly and the Kid stepped behind him to remove his gun.

"This should be interesting," the Kid said.

Clint could tell by the look on Hammer's face that Trap was in position. He assumed from that that the Kid was also positioned. With Hammer's life out of danger, he felt much more confident about matters.

"What do you say, Granger?" Clint said. "Let's see the famous Tenderhands move."

"It'll be the last thing you ever see," Granger said.

Clint waited, his hand hanging by his side. His muscles were tensed, his eyes alert, watching for telltale signs that he was going to go for his gun.

Granger flexed his gloved hand at his side. He'd been hired to do a job and the Gunsmith had embarrassed him by getting the herd through.

For that the man had to die.

Tenderhands moved for his gun and Clint knew immediately that the man's rep was all hype. Oh, he was fast, all right, but nowhere near as fast as his reputation had made him out to be.

Another example of how reputations are simply a lie.

It was no contest.

THIRTY-SIX

When they made love Clint was tender, and gentle. It had only been ten days since Beverly had been shot, and her shoulder was far from healed. It was she, however, who insisted that they share a bed that night.

He told her to stay on her back and let him do all the work. She closed her eyes and sighed as his mouth touched her breasts, his tongue teased her nipples, his hand slid between her legs and his skillful fingers brought her to gushing readiness.

He moved down, then, so that he could smell her fragrance and taste her tartness and she moaned, reaching for his head with her right hand. Her left arm, the injured one, remained at her side.

She wrapped the fingers of her right hand in his hair and lifted her hips as his tongue darted in and out of her, then slid upward and found her turgid clit. He circled it with his tongue, drew on it with his lips and brought her to a violent climax, then raised himself above her and entered her, sliding easily past her slick portal, plunging to the core of her hot, wet depths . . .

After two weeks Beverly pronounced herself ready to ride home . . . and Clint announced that he would not be accompanying her.

"I didn't think you would be," she said. "I don't know how to thank you, Clint. Getting that herd delivered has really gotten me out of trouble."

They were at the livery, both with their horses saddled and ready to leave. Clint helped her astride Lancelot, then mounted Duke. They rode outside together.

Clint knew that when Beverly returned to Wyoming Crandall would still be after her spread, but at least she wouldn't have to worry about the man called Tenderhands. Granger was dead, and Cantey and McKenzie had left town immediately after. Crandall would have to find himself some new boys.

As they hit the main street where Beverly's men were waiting for her she said, "Well, I guess I'll have to deal with Crandall all over again when I get home."

"I'm sure your new foreman will be able to handle anything Crandall can throw at you."

As he said it they pulled up aside her new foreman, Fred Hammer.

"You ready, Mrs. Press?"

"Ready, Hammer."

Clint reached across Beverly to shake hands with Hammer.

"Take good care of her, Hammer."

"I'll do my best, Clint."

He kissed Beverly and she touched his cheek tenderly.

"Don't wait until you need a horse to come and see me."

"I won't."

Hammer and Beverly urged their horses forward and their men followed. Clint watched until they were out of sight, then turned in his saddle to see Trap and the Kid riding up to him.

"You fellas leaving, too?"

"Nothing left to stay in this town for," the Kid said. "Trap used up all the women and won all the money."

"Sounds like you need greener pastures."

"Got someplace in mind?" Trap asked.

"I might," Clint said. "We can talk about it . . . after we talk about you boys."

"What about us?" Trap asked as all three urged their horses forward.

"Well, for starters," Clint said, "what the hell does 'Trap' mean?"

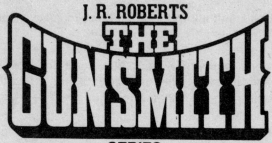

J. R. ROBERTS
THE GUNSMITH

SERIES